Praise for Mollie Hardwick and her previous mysteries

Malice Domestic
"A charming debut . . . [A] beguiling landscape of a sleepy little village."
—*The Baltimore Sun*

Parson's Pleasure
"Hardwick is an accomplished writer."
—*Library Journal*

Perish in July
"Hardwick again writes about believable characters coping not only with murder and other disasters but with a true-to-life marriage."
—*Publishers Weekly*

The Bandersbatch
"A quintessential cozy."
—*The Denver Post*

UNEASEFUL DEATH

Mollie Hardwick

FAWCETT CREST • NEW YORK

A Fawcett Crest Book
Published by Ballantine Books
Copyright © 1988 by Mollie Hardwick

Library of Congress Catalog Card Number: 87-38258

ISBN 0-449-22030-3

This edition published by arrangement with St. Martin's Press, Inc.

Manufactured in the United States of America

First Ballantine Books Edition: July 1993

For
JOHN KEATS
(1795–1821),
from whose writings all
chapter headings are taken,
and who kindly supplied the plot.

Chapter 1

Bitter chill it was

"St. Agnes's Eve," said Doran.

"What is?" Rodney was deep in the minutes of the last Annual Parochial Church Meeting. He frowned and pushed his spectacles up and down as he read over and over the reports on the election of sidepersons, proposals for the raising of money for the Organ Fund, and the incomprehensibly devious proceedings of the area Deanery Synod.

"The Roadshow. At Caxton Manor. Beginning on 20 January. Which happens to be St. Agnes's Eve, tomorrow," Doran said, slowly and clearly. "I just thought you'd like to know."

Rodney raised his head, a reminiscent smile that heralded a burst of quotation spreading over his pleasant features.

"Ah, bitter chill it was," he began. *"The hare limped trembling through the frozen grass, And silent was the flock in woolly fold . . ."*

"Yes, well," his wife interrupted hastily. Keats's poem had some forty-two stanzas, all of which he was capable of reciting from his phenomenal memory. It seemed a shame to stem the flow of recitation which gave him so much pleasure, but it would take him the whole evening to get through the task before him, which by rights he should not have been doing at all.

On their wedding day, just over four months ago, he had broken the news to his bride that he was thinking of leaving

1

the Church's ministry. He had long been unhappy under the new régime which had robbed the Church of its old, gracious language, reducing the Bible and the Liturgy to something little more distinguished than the minutes through which he was struggling. He was fond of his beautiful old church, St. Crispin's in the Kentish village of Abbotsbourne, set in an equally beautiful valley beneath the gentle rise of the Downs. But he felt, and had told his Bishop, that he was not the right vicar for Abbotsbourne: possibly not for anywhere. He was thirty-nine, still young enough for a new start in a different profession.

Surprisingly, particularly after the somewhat scandalous adventure he and Doran had shared the previous summer, involving two murders, the solution to a series of daring antiques robberies, and their own excursion into unmarried bliss, the church authorities had not shown any eagerness to get rid of him. He was popular in the village, liked for his kindness and patience with the most trying parishioners, and for what they thought of as an endearing dottiness, his habit of introducing into his sermons and conversation lines, sometimes whole verses, of poetical works completely unknown to them, often from most obscure authors.

And they had been sorry for him in his long widowerhood, coping with his young daughter Helena, the victim of a muscular disease. Helena was difficult, everybody agreed. A less loving father would have her put into a Home: the Reverend Chelmarsh had tolerated her possessiveness and violent tempers with untiring affection, and bought her an extremely expensive self-propelled invalid chair.

The parish had been pleased when he had married again. Everybody had known, of course, that he and Doran Fairweather were sweet on each other. Their unofficial holiday together in the Cotswolds had certainly caused a bit of talk, after the local policeman's son had leaked the news of it, but after all you're only young once, and he hadn't done anything half as bad as what you read in the papers about vicars who ought to be downright ashamed of themselves. And the new Mrs. Chelmarsh was a nice girl, pretty if you admired the slender, airy-fairy type, and clever—what she didn't know about old things wasn't worth knowing, not surprising when you remembered she ran that antique shop at Eastgate, the seaside town a few miles away.

People still tended to call her Miss Fairweather, which she didn't mind at all, as she had kept the name for professional purposes. It was well known in the Trade, and she had a sneaking fondness for it as against Chelmarsh.

Rodney sighed heavily over Item 15, the Election of Auditors to the Parish Council.

"Old Jackson's firmly dead, and Ernest Tilman won't be talked out of resigning—doesn't get enough golf for a bank manager, I imagine. So who else do we find? Who else can even add two and two?"

"Don't look at me. My books would be permanently in the red if Howell didn't deal with them." Howell Evans was her partner in the shop, a Welshman as sharp and unscrupulous as Doran was dreamy and honest. "Anyway, why should you worry? Let them sort it out themselves. You'll be leaving soon, anyway."

"Now there's a pious hope, if I may use the phrase. The man they'd got to replace me down with double pneumonia, and his physicians advising him that this part of the world's too cold for a delicate creature like him, and he ought to look for a living in Cornwall or the Scillies or somewhere? *Do* physicians still advise patients? *Physician Nature! let my spirit blood* . . . Keats ought to have known better than to suggest such a thing, as a medical man himself. And speaking of Keats, what's all this about St. Agnes's Eve?"

"I told you. But never mind, finish what you're doing."

Rodney slammed the sheaf of paper down on a side table, took off his spectacles, polished them, and stared at her defiantly. She thought, not for the first time, how much she liked his eyes, brown with a green tinge, moss-agate, slanted down at the outer corners: dark-lashed and warm with love and liking whenever they met hers. It was said that honeymoon glamour soon wore off, but in her experience that was untrue.

"I shan't finish it," Rodney declared. "Not now. I shall do the wretched thing tomorrow, directly after breakfast, when I'm fresh. Let it stew in its own boring juice. Why don't we watch the cricket?"

He switched on the television, whose screen showed them strangely clad figures dashing about in Australian sunshine on an expanse of emerald grass. "Move up," he said.

Doran made room for him on the sofa, where they sat close, her head against his shoulder, her hand in his. Even without the cricket it was a good way to spend an evening. Rodney sniffed appreciatively the fragrance of her hair, which she washed with a herbal shampoo from the Nature Shop in the village, having heard that some commercial varieties were tested in laboratories on rabbits' eyes. The hair itself was short, soft and brown, growing in natural curls. Rodney supposed it was what poets meant by hyacinthine. He looked down at her delicate pensive profile as she contemplated the cunning grace of a spin bowler.

"How very odd they look in blue and yellow, with stripes," she mused.

"*The run-stealers flicker to and fro, to and fro.* In white flannels, because they were ghosts, of course. Certainly not in blue and yellow with stripes. Never mind, it's nice to be watching sunshine in January."

The wicket fell. The face of the television commentator suddenly filled the screen and announced that viewers could join him again tomorrow. Rodney switched off. "So much for the Antipodes. Go on about Caxton Manor."

"Well. It's a stately home, or rather it was, because it's

4

been turned into a stately country house hotel. There was a house there in John Evelyn's time, late seventeenth century. It goes back long before that, but the present house is mostly eighteenth and nineteenth century, typical Georgian with additions, rather nicely imitated.''

"Far away?"

"Quite near, cross-country, the other side of Ashford in what estate agents call a pleasant rural setting. Do say if I'm boring you.''

"Not at all. *My ear is open like a greedy shark:* Keats again. When do we get to St. Agnes's Eve?''

"Now. There's going to be an Antiques Roadshow at Caxton starting tomorrow, and I'm one of the experts. You look baffled. Don't tell me you've never watched the television Roadshow, hordes and hordes of people rolling up to various venues with their family treasures, grandma's milk-jug and the bit of scrimshaw Uncle Ernest's father brought back from a whaling expedition. Hidden riches in the attic.''

"Why? I mean, why do they roll up?''

"To get their treasures valued by experts,'' Doran explained patiently. "They hope they've got something worth thousands, and just once in a series somebody has. But it's all fascinating, even the junk. I can't think why you're asking me all this. Everybody's seen the Roadshow—they can't resist the chance of a great discovery coming up.''

Rodney said nothing. When he had lived at the vicarage it had been Helena who had dictated what they watched on television. She wasn't able to go about like other people, she said, so it was her right to be entertained at home. And because she hated Doran, her rival for Rodney's love, anything connected with antiques would instantly be switched off. He had refrained from mentioning this to Doran, so that the subject of the Roadshow had never come up in their limited time together before their marriage.

Now that they both lived at Bell House, Doran's home,

5

Helena no longer monopolized the television set. Doran had tackled the formidable task of taming her stepdaughter by beginning as she meant to go on.

"We all have rights," she pointed out. "Your father works, so he needs to watch things that relax his mind. I work, so the same applies to me. You don't work, but you need your amusements too, and any education there is going. So we have to share the viewing, obviously."

Helena pushed out her lip and tensed herself for an outburst of screams and tears. "I want a set of my own."

"Ah." Doran's tone was casual. "Well, as it happens, there's an old set in the cellar that my housekeeper used to watch, when I had a housekeeper. It's black and white and I can't guarantee the reception, but you're welcome to it. I'll have it brought up from the cellar."

After that there had been other storms, demands for the old set to be adjusted or that Helena be allowed to watch the one in the drawing room; accusations of selfishness and brutality. Doran had grimly let them wash over her, almost never letting the girl see the constant fraying of her nerves. She had known that life with Helena would be difficult—it was the reason why she had not married Rodney earlier. She had taken on a great challenge, and she would fight it out, for her own sake and Rodney's. And even Helena's.

Rodney turned the conversation away from television.

"Who are your companions in expertise in this breathless entertainment—your Eastgate pals?"

"Oh, if only they were—then I should know exactly what competition I'd have. As it is, they're going to be people from all over the place. I haven't been sent a list, but they're all specialists."

"You're a specialist."

"Not much of one. I've got a lovely collection of fans because I really know about them, and how many super fans have survived the ravages of time? Fragile little things with

6

sticks that snap and silk that tears and feathers that fall out. Not a lot left in East Kent, I fear.''

"But there's your other stuff, isn't there?''

"Early pottery and porcelain and pictures. Also highly perishable. How I'd love to think that somebody would come trotting up to me with a David Cox landscape or a Louis Wain clowder of crazy cats, or an English delft charger or a Ralph Wood animal or a Bristol bottle in those lovely blues. I'd even be very happy to see a bit of unusual Staffs, *not* John Wesley and not badly repaired from a tube of DIY glue. But there won't be any. The trouble is, nice things are getting rarer and rarer.''

She looked around the room, furnished and decorated with objects she had been unable to part with, having originally bought them to re-sell. Some belonged to the period of the house, Queen Anne with older rooms at the back, some were much later and a very few pieces were earlier. They lived very amicably together. All had been hand-crafted with care, pride and affection in their time and seemed to have taken on shades of the personality of their makers. They despised, in silent elegance, any object which had slid off the assembly line. Among them, the television set looked sheepish.

Rodney, though no expert himself, enjoyed living with them and in the charming rooms of Bell House, after the ponderous grimness of the ugly vicarage, whose furniture matched its railway-station exterior. He sensed that Helena also preferred Bell House, though she wouldn't lower her pride to say so.

"Will there be anything in it for you?'' he asked Doran. "I mean, could you buy anything you liked?''

Doran looked surprised. "Goodness. I suppose I could if it was in my price range. In fact, there are ways . . .'' She stopped. It was kinder not to disillusion Rodney further about the Trade by letting him into a certain discreditable practice.

7

Anyway, this would not be that sort of roadshow. Or she hoped not.

"You won't," Rodney said, "be getting involved in anything shady—especially not in anything dangerous? We don't want a repetition of the Murderous Affair at Weller Green, do we? In fact, if there's any chance of it I shall put my foot down and forbid you to go. Or, more effectively, I shall have a diplomatic cold of fearful proportions and you'll have to stay at home and nurse me."

Doran kissed his cheek. "Don't worry. Antique dealing doesn't come with a built-in government health warning—quite a lot of people engage in it without getting murdered, or even attacked. What happened in the Cotswolds was most exceptional."

"I hope so," Rodney said grimly, "I hope so. I still have nightmares about that vault."

The door opened and Helena's electric wheelchair glided in, with Helena in it. Her sharp dark eyes went to the television screen, but it was blank: she could not level any accusations of self-indulgence about that.

She was almost fourteen, smaller than she should have been because of the disease that had wasted her body. Her spine had not grown straight, her shoulders were slightly hunched, and her limbs were bonier than a child's should be. But her thin face had a certain elfin attraction: Rodney could see in it something of his dead wife Benita. Out of the corner of his eye he saw Doran preparing herself for battle.

"Oh, good," she said brightly. "Come and sit by the fire." By unspoken agreement she and Rodney moved apart.

Helena slammed the door shut behind her and propelled her chair almost onto the hearthrug. "I have to, haven't I. It's freezing in my room." She occupied ground-floor rooms in the oldest, Carolean part of the house, a bedroom and a sitting room. They were small, cosy and as attractive as Doran's impeccable taste could make them.

8

"Hardly freezing, surely," Doran said. "The radiators are turned full up. Have you finished your homework?"

Helena scowled. She had put up a violent resistance to being sent to day school, a small private establishment just outside Abbotsbourne. But Doran had insisted on it. Home care by nurse-housekeepers had not been a success, the lessons given by a young teacher from the local comprehensive school had been of limited use. Helena was intelligent, and pride compelled her to learn enough to avoid appearing a fool, but it was not the sort of pride which drove her to distinguish herself. It was clear to Doran that the girl needed competition and the company of her peers. With a firmness that astonished Rodney, she drove Helena to Craiglands School every morning and collected her every afternoon, ignoring tears, tantrums and finally sullen silence. And it was working: almost imperceptibly it was working, on one level.

"No, I haven't finished my homework. The geography's too difficult, and you didn't come to help me, Daddy. Anyway, I don't see why I should have to do homework, it's slave-driving."

Doran stayed silent. Rodney must fight his own skirmishes.

"If slaves worked hard enough they sometimes finished up as freemen," he said. "Their masters used solemnly to unfasten the iron collars they wore round their necks and shake hands with them. Then they could drop their slave names and call themselves what they liked. This was in Norman times, of course—the slaves were mostly Saxon and immensely superior people."

"I know," Helena said surprisingly. "They made beautiful jewellery. Torques and bracelets and brooches, out of pewter and bronze and gold and silver, with precious stones set in them, much better than people made later. Miss Em-

9

erson says there was a Saxon treasure-hoard dug up outside Henbury.''

"I should like to see that," said Doran, who had seen it often.

"Oh, you could if you bothered to go to Barminster Museum," Helena told her loftily. We're going there in a coach after Easter. At least, I shall go if I'm well enough," she added hastily, having forgotten to slip in a grumble. "Annabella will look after me," she added, a touch smugly.

"Who's Annabella?" Rodney asked.

"My best friend. A *Senior.* She's sixteen. She's brilliant."

Rodney forebore to glance at Doran. They had never heard Helena refer to anyone as brilliant before, or believed her capable of such a sentiment.

Doran took the opportunity of Helena's unwonted graciousness to break the news that she would be going away for two nights. "But Carole will be here to look after you." Carole Flesher was a young married woman from the council estate who "obliged" at Bell House with extra duties when required. Always willing to earn an extra penny, she would stay the night on occasion. Doran refused to impose on Rodney the strain of sole responsibility for Helena.

"I don't like Carole. Why can't Vi come?"

"Because Vi works for so many other people and she gets tired. It isn't fair to ask her. Besides, Carole has two children of her own, and she's done a bit of nursing." No, that had been the wrong thing to say, better not to remind Helena of her invalidism.

"I might be ill," Helena suggested eagerly. "Then Vi would be much better for me. If I want my back rubbed she doesn't hurt."

"Neither will Carole, and I'm sure she's good for you." In fact Doran did not care greatly for Carole, a tight-lipped and somewhat cold-seeming girl who, though highly efficient, always seemed to have her mind on something else.

Vi Small, domestic help to so many villagers, was warm and cheerful, and gossiped agreeably. Tall, strong, handsome if no longer young, Vi was Abbotsbourne's favourite household goddess.

"Vi's better at back-rubbing than you are." Helena flung a gratuitous dart. "Are you only going for two nights?"

"I'm afraid so." It was hard to resist sarcasm. "Of course, if I can spin it out I will."

Rodney began to speak, but Doran stopped him with a look. This was a contest of Amazons. Weary of it, he went back to his parish notes, leaving Doran to see Helena back to her room, where he knew the contest would continue over geography homework.

When Doran returned her cheeks were pink, as much from rigorous self-control as from the effort of pitting her will against Helena's. She reached for her sewing basket and began to work unenthusiastically at a cross-stitch design on canvas, which at some distant time, with luck, would cover a church kneeler.

They sat in silence. At times like this she wished, in spite of her love for Rodney, that she had not married him: that she was still living alone and free, with no alien presence in the house, no sense that she was being resented and silently cursed. Helena had asked her the same question as Rodney's, but with very different intent: "Do you think anyone will get murdered when you go away this time, like last year? Ben Eastry said someone tried to kill you and bury you, and the police found a body."

"Ben Eastry talks too much, especially for a policeman's son. Well, I did go to Swansea and Cardiff on a buying trip a few weeks ago, and nothing happened to me there. So far as I know Caxton Manor is a highly respectable place. Sorry to disappoint you. You can read for exactly a quarter of an hour, and then I shall come and put your light out." She

11

tried not to see Helena's smile of triumph at having drawn blood.

It was hard, when one was not yet twenty-eight and without vanity knew oneself to be attractive, to have to behave like a cross between a dragonish Victorian governess and an early Christian keeping silent under the lash of the Roman scourge. She found it a relief to drive to her shop, then to the pub where she and Howell met their dealer friends. Some of them were not exactly friends in the best sense, but at least they weren't invaders on one's home ground. Home was a sacred place: that was why being burgled upset people far above the value of their property.

She was looking forward with ashamed eagerness to going to the Manor. For two days and nights she would be among civilized company, people who spoke her language, who would be prepared to like her and respect her judgement. For that blessed, all too short time, she would not have to be with Helena.

Rodney glanced up. "Can I tell the Young Wives' Club that you'd be prepared to give them a talk? On affordable antiques, objects they can buy themselves, that sort of thing? Mrs. Kenney says they'd be simply fascinated."

"Who wouldn't? Yes, of course I'll talk to them, so long as it's an evening. I'll even join if they'd like that. *You* would, wouldn't you?"

"Well . . . yes, it would be nice." Rodney had nobly refrained from trying to turn Doran into an archetypal vicar's wife, but it would certainly be an advantage to him to have one who attended parish meetings. "I'll tell her. Thank you, my darling." He forebore to say that he had had a similar request from the Mothers' Union. Doran, with Helena for a stepdaughter, would not contemplate maternity. They had discussed it once, agreeing never to mention it again. The discussion had been emotional.

But Doran now broke the rules, cruelly. She knew all too

12

well how much Rodney would have liked a child of their own, a normal child. "Not the MU as well, I presume?"

Rodney kept his eyes on the minutes. "No." After a moment he raised them. "I don't think it's very fair of you to bring that up."

"And I don't think it's very fair of you to let me have all the disciplining of Helena to do. You might at least take over sometimes in the evenings, when she's at her worst."

"I do what I can. It's obviously not my place to put her to bed, at her age."

"Possibly not. But you could just look in when you know she's likely to snipe at me as she did just now. I do have my feelings, you know, unlikely as it may seem, and at this moment I feel very unwanted and uncomfortable—in my own home."

"I back you up all I can."

"Oh yes, when you can bring yourself to speak sharply to your precious spoiled infant. Speaking of which, you can hardly blame me for not wanting a child of my own when I've got a stepchild like that one."

Then they were having a row, a scene such as they had never had before. All the self-control, the forbearance on both sides, broke down into anger and recriminations, as though they were not Doran and Rodney but strangers and enemies. Suddenly, hearing herself shouting, Doran turned sharply away from him.

"That's enough. We're both behaving disgracefully. Let's call a truce, shall we? I want a drink. What about you?"

"No thanks." He sat down and returned to his paperwork while Doran poured a brandy for herself, hearing the hiss of the soda-siphon as loudly as a waterfall, hearing a log fall from the grate: tiny sounds in the cold silence that was between them. She remembered that as a child, after a scolding by her mother, she had felt the same, all her senses heightened by the disturbance of anger and fear. It was adrenalin at work, probably. We are all savages under the layers, she thought, primitive little creatures bracing up for flight at the approaching roar of the sabre-toothed tiger: if that animal was roaming the plains at the same time as early Man. She turned to ask Rodney, but what she could see of his face was too formidable for nonsense. She noticed the increased grey among the brown of his hair. So that was what marriage to her had done, was it?

After what seemed hours he replaced the parish minutes in a file, shut it and crowned it with a valuable Cliché millefiori paperweight forcibly enough to make Doran nervous for the precious thing.

Summoning a falsely bright voice, she said, "You oughtn't to have gone back to that stuff tonight, after all. You're not making much impression on it, are you?"

He answered in a cold, detached tone, very unlike his usual one, *"As the partridge sitteth upon eggs, and hatcheth them not."*

Good, at least he could still throw in a quote. "That doesn't sound like Keats."

"No. Jeremiah, Prophet of Lamentations. I'm tired, I'm going to bed. Good night."

When he had gone Doran poured herself another drink and looked back on the ruined evening. *I was angry with my friend; I told my wrath, my wrath did end.* Well, so it had done. But something had happened between them that would not be forgotten.

Chapter 2

Who are these coming to the sacrifice?

The morning of 20 January did not so much dawn as reveal itself slowly and reluctantly. So far as it was concerned, thought Doran, glancing out into the paling blackness, the night might just as well not have bothered to end. At least there was neither snow nor frost, merely a cold mirk. St. Agnes's Eve, ah, bitter chill it was. Still true.

Breakfast was a hurried unsociable function, Rodney reading up his work of the previous night as he ate, a habit Doran had tried to discourage. The shadow of the night before was still between them. The usual rush to get Helena to school followed, her folding portable wheelchair packed into the car, her homework briefcase brought from her room, woollen gloves which had vanished tracked down to the cat's basket, where they had become hopelessly matted with black hairs.

"See you later," Doran called, on her way out.

"I'll be at the vicarage," Rodney answered. The Barminster authorities had made it clear that they preferred him to do as much parish work in the still-vacant house as possible, rather than at the home he had frivolously chosen.

"Oh, all right, I'll look in there before I leave."

When she reached the vicarage at a minute or so past nine Rodney was in conference with the vicar's warden, Bill Gregg, a large choleric-faced man whom Doran had never liked. She knew that the dislike was fully reciprocated, reinforced by disapproval of what Gregg considered to be her immoral character. Since she had wantonly decoyed his vicar into marriage he had barely spoken to her.

Rodney looked up from the table at which they were working. His vague glance implied that he had never seen her before, or only recognized her with difficulty. As briefly as possible she gave him last-minute instructions for the two days of her absence. He seemed more concerned with the collection of Helena from school and her evening régime than the fact that she, Doran, would be away.

"I really doubt if she'll dissolve or fall to pieces just because I'm not there," she said crisply. "With Carole in the house I can't see what can go wrong."

"Carole's not a very—well—caring girl, is she? Don't you think Vi—"

"No, I don't, and now I've made the arrangements they'll stand. Your food's all taken care of. If you need me in emergency you've got the number, but only in emergency, please. Right, I'm off."

"Good," said Rodney, not meaning that he was glad to see her go but because, with his mind on the bills for church heating, he could think of nothing else to say. Doran thought of giving him their usual parting kiss, decided against it, and almost ran out. Bill Gregg made a mental note to tell his wife that Mrs. Chelmarsh was not only wayward and no better than she should be but a proper little shrew, as his old mother would have said.

When Doran entered the kitchen it was immediately obvious to Vi that all was not well with her employer. Natural tact kept her from remarking on this. She had seen trouble coming in that house ever since the wedding. Gossip was as good a cure for bad moods as any she knew—it took your mind off your own affairs.

"Morning," she greeted Doran. "Nasty and cold, isn't it, but no snow yet. I see you've got your warm boots on, it pays to buy the best. Talking about that, you know her next door?"

16

She could only mean Richenda Berg, the glamorous model wife of the equally glamorous Cosmo, a sort of international jet-set marketeer.

"Mrs. Berg. What about her? She's away winter-sporting isn't she?"

Vi's handsome features arranged themselves into an expression of profound knowledge and wisdom.

"Ah, but who with, that's the question? Now Hayley, my friend that lives round the corner from me, you know who I mean, she and Dave had a ten-day Christmas break on the Costa, and when they were coming back through Gatwick who should they see but Her?"

"Well, not surprising—"

"Got up like something out of Dallas, all in white fur with a lot of skiing stuff on a trolley and that brown shiny makeup, laughing and talking. And it wasn't Him with her but a young man not half her age, Hayley reckoned, ever so good-looking. They looked very close, if you know what I mean." Vi piled up clean plates with emphasis.

"Perhaps it was her brother, seeing her off," Doran suggested feebly.

"Brother? He was nearly as dark as a Spanish boy, Hayley said, and she ought to know having just come from there—she got really quite friendly with a wine waiter at their hotel, not that there was anything in it, just one of those holiday things and Dave isn't the jealous type. But it was funny, though, wasn't it, seeing her at Gatwick. . . ."

"Very strange." Doran fully appreciated that Vi's tattle had been a deliberate piece of kindness. A current of warm understanding passed between them. "Well. I must be on my way. I don't know the route too well and I want to be there in good time for lunch."

They discussed food preparation and other necessary arrangements. As Doran was about to go upstairs for her luggage a tap at the door announced the arrival of Carole. She was a small, neat girl with a slender figure and a face which would have been attractive if she had let herself smile more. Her ash-blonde hair was hidden by a knitted tea-cosy hat, her legs encased in thin cheap boots of a startling petunia pink, with high heels.

"Thought I'd look in and see everything was fixed up," she said, with the brusque nod which was all the greeting Doran ever got from her.

"Oh, it is, to the last detail, Carole. Vi will tell you. You know about Helena's pills, of course. Oh, and don't let her read too long after she's gone to bed."

"I won't." Nor you will, thought Doran, consciously glad to be handing Helena over to this slightly grim young person who would stand no nonsense. As she drove away from Bell House in the roomy Volvo estate car which had replaced her old saloon she knew all the sensations of a released prisoner stepping into freedom through the small doorway so familiar to viewers of police dramas. The car was known as Harris, a name which reminded Doran fondly of their Cotswold adventure, when she and Rodney had passed themselves off as the Reverend and Mrs. Richard Harris Barham.

The familiar lanes began to drop behind her, and their associations of occasions, words, laughs. Here we were saying . . . that corner was where Rodney remembered . . . we used to call that cottage with the crooked chimney the Hexelhaus . . . at that corner he used to say "The legions had to march single-file, even in those days." Things remembered in the past tense, as though she-and-he were people in an old story.

Then the motorway was opening up, wide and impersonal, a road that led nowhere and anywhere, ancient velvet-turfed hill forts on one side, industrial blisters on the other, until great blaring London signs began to appear. There was no great haste, in spite of what she said to Vi; the haste had been to get away from home. She took a southerly exit to cross the sluggish little river Stour and wander round villages which managed to keep their sturdy prettiness even against bilious leaden skies, among gardens whose trees and shrubs were only blackened lifeless twigs. The whole countryside wore a monochrome look, like a faded old film.

January, the Wolf-month, the Aefter-Yule of the Saxons. It suited Doran's mood perfectly. She was aware now of other things besides the storm that had broken over her. For one thing, she was cold. Inside the hood of her coat, lined with thick fake fur, her ears were chilly; her hands felt numb in the lined driving gloves. The car's heater was inadequate. Doran wished that Howell were with her, and the flat bottle which always accompanied him on their buying trips. If only a wayside restaurant were open, or a pub.

Then she saw the sign: Coffee. A pub was indeed open, long before licensing hours allowed, for the sale of non-alcoholic refreshments. She was shown to a seat by a powerful electric fire and given a cup of coffee of equal strength, strong enough to banish the memory of last night's brandy and breakfast's almost untasted tea. From that moment her spirits began to rise. Or, more accurately, despondency slumped to the floor of her mind. She hoped it would pull a blanket over its head and stay there.

Off the motorway, hastily past what the spoilers had done to the old market town of Ashford, she was on a wide busy road that eventually led to Maidstone. Turning off it, she was back in rural Kent, stark open prospects whose summer loveliness was as hidden now as though the Sleeping Beauty had retired to a bed in a mud mask and a shroud of grey. Here and there a field of sheep cropped thoughtfully.

Twice Harris lost his way and once was nearly bisected by a transport careering down a hill towards a hairpin bend. An alluring cobbled square and a delectable church slowed down the car's pace, while Doran debated whether to stop and explore the church's interior, since the door was open.

Rodney and his churchwardens had a running battle about leaving the door in St. Crispin's south porch unlocked. He said that a church was there for people to go into when they needed spiritual refreshment of any kind. They contended that an open door invited visitors who were not so much in search of spiritual refreshment as of church plate and the contents of offertory boxes. This had proved painfully true in some local churches, and Abbotsbourne's had a particularly sumptuous and portable mediaeval triptych. The churchwardens won.

Spiritual refreshment would have been as welcome to Doran as the recent coffee, but the shade of Keats reminded her what churches were like in cruel January. *The sculptur'd dead on each side seem to freeze . . . and his weak spirit fails, To think how they may ache in icy hoods and mails.* No, perhaps it wasn't a day for inspecting the sculptur'd dead. She drove on, and came within minutes to a modest signboard proclaiming the entrance to Caxton Manor.

A long carriage road snaked its way through gently undulating grounds where more silent flocks regarded Doran with a gaze peculiar to sheep, a blend of apathy and disapproval. Ahead the house stood waiting, a Georgian manor plain but comely, two substantial wings flanking a porticoed centre.

Cars were parked around it, ranging from a sleek BMW to a popular make which appears with great frequency in crime reports. Doran parked Harris, inspected her reflection, grimaced at it for its unbecoming pink nose and a certain heaviness of eye, and locked Harris.

The portico led straight into a spacious hall. Doran did a lightning calculation of the changes it must have gone through in its life, including Tudor and Edwardian. At the moment it was occupied by a great many people milling about with drinks in their hands: the unmistakable roar of a cocktail party had been audible far off. She knew that a number of locals had been invited to meet the experts.

A stunningly handsome young man in what looked like a Victorian footman's uniform appeared, Mercury-like, and took possession of Doran's overnight bag and coat before she could say who she was or ask where he was taking it. He seemed to know the first fact and to have a godlike disregard for the second.

An equally beautiful young woman in 1890s maid's uniform topped by a frilly streamered cap approached with a tray laden with glasses. She didn't quite perform the feat of curtseying while offering it, but somehow managed to convey the impression of doing so.

"A drink, madam?"

Madam was impressed that she was not expected to choose between red wine, white wine and sherry. The glass was the correct narrow flute shape, and beaded bubbles were winking at the brim. Keats may not have known that this phenomenon did not normally appear in beakers full of the true, the blushful Hippocrene, but it definitely appeared in champagne. Doran sipped gratefully, trying not to toss the whole glassful off at once.

Seen over the glass's rim, and after half its contents, the company present appeared splendidly exotic. Nobody was ostentatiously dressed. The house's earlier occupants would have thought these children of the second Elizabethan Age colourless, even drab. Yet there was colour, rich purples, blazing reds among the clothes of the women, evidence of style and taste among the men, flashes of gold and jewels on hands with sensitive tips and very clean nails.

And the odd uncouth figure to point up the elegance of the rest. Doran looked across to the cheerfully blazing log fire. Leaning casually against the imposing chimneypiece was her business partner, Howell Evans.

A short, stocky man whose dark facial stubble was imperfectly shaved, Howell was nobody's elegance symbol. Georgians would have assumed him to be a groom strayed

21

in from the stables. Doran was quite disproportionately glad to see him. She made her way to his side.

"Hello, louse. What on earth are you doing here?"

"Me? An expert, amn't I?" His Welsh accent, deliberately stronger than usual, caused heads to turn.

"Well, yes. But you weren't invited—were you?"

"Not to say invited, no. But I thought you could do with a bit of 'elp, bein' on your own, and two heads is better than one." He was covertly eyeing her, taking in the signs of strain and the absence of the lamp of happiness which could make her large hazel eyes luminous. Though possessed of a hard exterior and a poorly developed bump of honesty, and having no fancy for women as women, Howell felt for Doran an affection and a loyalty far beyond anything he felt for the sequence of young men who had been his partners in another sense. It was never mentioned on either side, but both knew it was there. He considered her weak, of poor judgement, too soft in a bargain; but she was his partner, his *cydymaith*, and if anyone were to cause her harassment, aggro or pain, he would fight for her as he had fought in boyhood in the cobbled streets of his Welsh valley town.

In his opinion someone had caused her pain recently, and he would have betted the blue-dash charger which he had just acquired for a song on the identity of that person.

"Of course I'm delighted to have your support," Doran said. "So long as they know you're here."

"That's all right, I squared 'em. Said I didn't mind tacklin' any odds and ends nobody else wanted. Like common furniture—bound to be some rubbish—and silver a specialty. Their silver man's let them down, did you know? Tibetan flu or some bug. I'd 've offered myself for clocks but they've got someone else, rot 'em, guy called Chance or Dance or whateffer." He emptied his tankard (how had he got hold of beer when everyone else was drinking champagne?) and told her about the blue-dash charger, a very nice Adam and Eve sub-

22

ject, and about the skeleton clock, shaped like Lincoln Cathedral, which someone had brought in, under the impression that it was unfinished and of no value.

"Just walked in off the street with it. Nasty ugly thing, she said, Granny was ever so fond of it, but it gave her the abdabs, watchin' time tick away like that, seemed to make life shorter, and why hadn't they put a proper front on it? Up towards the thousand, that could make," he said happily, "with a good clean and overhaul."

"Howell! You didn't tell her? You let her think it was . . . how much did you give her?"

He glanced aside. "Plenty. She was just an old biddy, you know. Don't you look at me like that, gal. You may think I'm a tight-wad but I'm fair."

Doran shook her head despairingly. "We won't argue about it now. I'll have a look when we get back on Thursday. Who's that man, the very tall one over there by the pillar? I know his face, don't I?"

"Should. He's been on the box enough times. Falk Lydgate, antiquities—Greek, Roman, Egyptian, thinks medieval's vulgarly modern. But they've asked him for Furniture, because he's pretty hot on that, too, and there's not a lot of classical remains likely to turn up."

"Fork? Extraordinary name."

"F—a—l—k. Don' ask me where you get a name like that. Rum sort of bird."

The man had, indeed, a birdlike appearance, with a head smallish in proportion to his long body, thick fair hair, greying, rising in a steep crest, a long neck bent down now towards his shorter companion, a beakish nose and haughtily drooping eyelids. Yet there was something not unhandsome, not ignoble, about the face, as though he had absorbed some essence of grandeur from laurelled heads on coins and busts of the Caesars. Doran remembered him now, and knew what his voice would be like without being able to hear it over the

23

party noise: dry, precise, donnish. She failed to recognize any of the other faces. Probably, like her, they were small dealers with some specialist knowledge. One young blonde woman, as sweetly pretty as a Jumeau doll, with a hint of cuddly commonness, was pointed out as an expert on antique firearms, Mrs. Mercia Lang. It seemed unlikely, but in the trade anything was possible. Doran thought she detected something faintly unpleasant about that apple-blossom face: weakness, depravity?

A large man who could have been a beef farmer proved to be an expert on that most fragile of substances, antique glass. It seemed not merely unlikely but impossible, with those big red hands. Howell, who had been finding things out on his own behalf, volunteered the information that he was Bert Prinn of Northampton.

"Bert. How on earth can he have got christened Albert, only—forty years or so or thereabouts? It just wasn't a fashionable name any more."

"Matter of fact," Howell said with his tomcat grin, "he wasn't. Believe it or not, his name's Ethelbert. Parents must have been ravin' loonies, he's been tryin' to live it down ever since. But somebody found out and he keeps gettin' ribbed about it."

"Yes, he would, wouldn't he? If I get intimate with him I must remember not to refer to it."

Howell gave her a suspicious glance. "Not thinkin' of gettin' intimate with any of these guys, are you? I can tell you're up for grabs. Don't you go gettin' into no trouble, will you."

"Howell! Sometimes I don't know why I bother with anyone as rude as you. I'm *not* up for grabs, and anyway, it's none of your business. By the way, how interesting that both those people have Anglo-Saxon names. She's a Saxon kingdom and he's a Saxon king—of Kent, I rather think. Unusual." And strange, after the conversation with Rodney and Helena yesterday . . .

She left Howell and moved about the hall. It was necessary to look where one was going, since it was strewn with the minutiae of an Edwardian country house. Two huge yellow Labradors sprawled in luxurious coma before the fire, a pair of riding boots, still muddy, stood near the hearth, a whip leaned up against a shabby leather-topped music stool, a coat-rack of extreme hideousness bore an inverness coat, a tweed cape, a bowler hat with a curly brim, and a topper which had lost its shine. At any moment, Doran felt, the stately form of Lord Ribblesdale might stalk through the door, elegantly attired for the hunt as painted by Sargent in 1902.

Since everybody seemed to be too busy talking to notice her she went back to Howell.

"I've been doing a quick estimate of everything in the room," she said.

"Yeh? And?"

"Of course you know already. There's nothing really pinchable enough to interest anyone but a kleptomaniac."

"Go on."

"The lanterns. Very pretty coloured cathedral glass, but a bit damaged and too big for domestic use. The photographs are in what look like silver frames, but they're not, they're spelter or Britannia metal or something."

"Who are they of, anyway?"

"How should I know? Possibly assorted dead dukes and duchesses, but they could be anybody's relations from a photograph album. The ornaments, if that's the word, are imposing but junk. I bet you," she warmed to her subject, "that if you slipped anything in your pocket you'd find when you got it home that there was something wrong with it. That is if it was small enough to slip in your pocket." She eyed a looming statue of a Chinese god, made of plaster and certainly not in China. "See that Sunbonnet School picture up there—creeper-clad cottage, ducks, geese, little girl with kitten, the lot?"

"Just like what you sold two years ago to that guy in Manchester."

"For peanuts," said Doran bitterly. "Don't remind me. This one *could* be an Allingham, or an Emily Stannard the Third. But—"

"It's a print. Soap commercial."

"Right. But I don't know why I'm bothering to tell you, when you know it all."

"Well, stands to reason, when Joe Public's going to come trampin' in bright and early tomorrow. Wouldn't want real valuables about, would they? Clever."

"Very. I think the effect's terrific. Oh dear, we should circulate, but I don't think there's anyone I want to talk to, not stone cold sober."

"Me neither. Unsociable, that's us, *merch*."

Doran had no objection to being addressed as Howell's daughter, unlikely as such a relationship was. A train of thought led her to ask, "How's Andrew?"

He glanced aside, moodily stirring one of the Labradors with a toe. Obviously it was not the moment to inquire into his domestic affairs. She had no intention of discussing her own, which she was keeping firmly at bay.

One of the Victorian maids, a living and breathing Doulton figurine, poured them both another drink. Doran realized that for the first time that day she was actually warm, feeling the heat of the room and the fire.

At that moment the door opened, admitting a chilly blast and three people.

The younger of the two men came in like an east wind, swift-moving, glancing about him, like a forest creature scenting danger. He was not very tall, thin to the point of emaciation, his high cheekbones seeming about to pierce the skin that covered them. His hair was an unusual shade of dark chestnut, curly and untidily ruffled—like Rodney's, thought Doran with a pang—his head beautifully shaped, his mouth long and mobile, the upper lip projecting slightly over the lower one. He reminded Doran strongly of someone, but of whom?

The woman who had entered before him reminded her of a whole gallery of portraits. Like Shakespeare's mistress, millions of strange shadows tended on her. A Chalon belle of the 1840s, stately, languid and lovely, full-throated and sleek-skinned. Mary, Queen of Scots, the long oval of her face impassive, pent in severe coif and high ruff, yet radiating an astounding fascination before which the artist had retired, defeated. An Odalisque by Ingres. And countless other fatal dark ladies.

What this luscious beauty wore was unnoticeable. As the man behind her tenderly slipped her coat from her shoulders she gave her head a little shake of freedom and bestowed a queenly smile on him. A long thick plait of shining hair, almost black, hung down her back like the hair of a St. Trinian's schoolgirl but with vastly different effect.

Doran tore her fascinated gaze away from this vision to the other newcomer. He was older than his companions, perhaps in his early fifties. His hair was thick and pure white, with blue bright eyes under heavy dark brows. The eyes were enhanced by costly, high-fashion spectacles. Doran admired men in spectacles.

But they were not the cause of her heart skipping a beat. For Henry Gore was the man with whom, in the days of her apprenticeship to the antiques trade and to the painful process of growing up, she had briefly fallen in love.

Chapter 3

So many, and so many, and such glee

It had not been a serious affair, or, properly, an affair at all.

She had been very young, very green, very raw, still smarting from a disastrous entanglement and her clumsy attempts to compensate for it by experimenting with unsuitable men. Henry Gore, twice her age, a highly respected figure in the art world, had come into the antiques shop where she worked in Oxford. He had been attracted, she dazzled. Twice he had taken her out to dinner: the second time she had boldly invited herself back to his hotel room, where he had very gently and charmingly made it clear that he had no intention of taking advantage of her young ardour.

And that had been the end of it. She looked back now on the episode as though it had happened to a different person. But Henry was just the same, if possible even more attractive with the added years.

He saw her at once and came directly to her, pushing through a crowd of designer sweaters. Two large warm hands enclosed hers.

"Doran! Of all people. Doran Fairweather. It's been a long time."

"Henry. Yes, it has. You look well—in fact you look smashing, as though you'd just come from tropic climes." If she were not careful she would begin to stammer.

"I have—at least from Mexico, if you call that tropic.

Looking at Aztec figures. Just let me get rid of this coat and we'll go into a corner and talk.''

Which they did, and were still talking when the summons to lunch came. In the gracious dining room, where a scatter of small tables each seating four people awaited them, they chose a place by a window, fairly secluded. Henry had at once noted her wedding ring. With the tact she remembered he sensed that she was glad to be away from home and was not anxious to talk about it. Instead he talked himself, lightly, always keeping her in the forefront of the topic. What a blessing that he hadn't become a bore.

"Of course I remember what I was doing in Oxford that summer. Looking at European stuff in the Ashmolean, but I got seduced by the Arundel Marbles. In fact we went to see them together, didn't we?''

"We did, because there was a marble bust in the shop—''

"Head of a child, early second century AD, and you thought it might be one of the Collector Earl's pieces that had gone astray, as, alas, so many of them did.''

"About half, thanks to blasted Cromwell and his thugs.'' A voice interrupted.

"Nobody sittin' here?'' Anybody but Howell would have said, "Mind if I join you?'' but he was already seated and briskly spreading his napkin. The talk became general. Howell was impressed by the presence of a Name like Henry Gore, behaved himself and talked amusingly. But Doran was conscious of disappointment, and ashamed of herself for it. She had been glad to have Howell's company, and now she wished he would go away because she was even gladder to have Henry's. His courtesy, unforced charm and unvoiced admiration worked on her bruised spirit like a balm.

The dining room filled up, delicious Victorian waitresses flitted about, faces that had been strange an hour ago began to seem familiar. Doran questioned Henry about the two who had arrived with him.

"Morven Cair and Dermid Scance. I brought them down in my car. She's mainly jewellery, but decorative items as well, he's clocks and watches."

"Are they—a couple?"

Henry deliberated. "Not what you'd call a couple. No. Dermid would very much like to be, and that's not giving away any secrets. But the divine Morven isn't easy to pin down. Or so I gather."

"You've tried?" What an unforgivable, oafish thing to say, she realized too late.

There was the slightest of pauses, the slightest of smiles.

"That's a leading question, my dear. However, it kindly suggests that my connoisseurship takes in women, and I thank you for the compliment. And yes, since you ask, I have tried, but not hard."

"You'd make a wonderful diplomat."

Howell was looking from one to the other.

"You on about that dark bird over there?" Howell interrupted. "Guy she's with never takes his eyes off her. He'll have his soup down his vest if he doesn't watch out."

Dermid Scance was, indeed, staring fixedly at the woman by his side. She was not speaking to him, was apparently gazing round the room, taking little notice of him. Doran thought he had a hungry look, and the hunger was not for food.

"She *is* rather divine-looking," Doran said to Henry. "Something classical? Juno? Venus?"

"*À sa proie attachée?* Rather the other way round, the prey attached to the goddess." Henry's tone was loftily pitying. Obviously he'd never suffered from being any goddess's prey.

"Somebody else can't take his eyes off her." Doran indicated the tall austere Falk Lydgate, two tables away from Morven Cair.

"Oh. My dreaded rival on the Antiquities side. *Not* my

favourite person. I can't think why the organizers asked us both, unless it was to see if we'd fight. I'd no idea he'd be here. At least our fields are different—he condescends to furniture, on occasion, and I condescend to . . . anything really ancient. You know.''

"No, I don't, not really. You're hardly likely to get any offerings found in Roman burials at a Roadshow.''

Henry looked embarrassed, for him. "Something brought home from foreign travels, perhaps? Egyptian tomb figures?''

"Well, you never know your luck.'' It was most unlike the eminent Henry to deal in what the Trade calls smalls. "Your non-friend Lydgate looks ruthless—is he?''

"Aren't we all, when it comes to the point?''

"I'm not. At least, I don't think so.''

"More's the pity,'' muttered Howell through a large mouthful of saddle of hare with grapes. Doran eyed his plate with disgust.

"How can you eat that, Howell! Poor little wild hare, chased to death.''

"Good old Welsh pastime, gal. *Llon yw calon pawb yr awrhon, Ond y scwarnog fechan fad*, you know. Folk song, that, pretty.''

"Well, I hope it chokes you.''

"Yeh? I suppose that halibut you're noshing swam into the net and gave itself up.''

"That's different. . . .''

"Children, children!'' Henry interposed mildly. Doran relaxed. It was odd how Henry had in a very short space of time adjusted to them, as though he had known Howell for years and had never been parted from Doran. Suddenly she wished that it were so.

When lunch was over the company dispersed, most to their rooms. Doran's, like all the bedrooms in the main house, had a theme, in this case Victoriana. It was called the Princess Louise Room, after Victoria's artistic daughter. A delicate mid-century walnut double bed was covered by what Doran recognized as a bedspread of Cluny lace of about the same period, hand-made in an intricate design; a crinoline chair wearing its original upholstery sat beside it; a mahogany corner whatnot held charming trifles of pottery. On the walls were portraits of the royal house of Saxe-Coburg-Gotha. She decided to price the entire room, piece by piece, as an exercise for tomorrow, but after a few minutes found herself too languid. The previous night had been unrestful, lying at the far edge of the ample four-poster she shared with Rodney, both resolved not to touch the other. And the champagne before lunch had been a good one.

She undressed partly and peeled back the Cluny bedspread. Below the pillows a hot-water bottle in a cosy knitted cover invited her. She joined it, and fell into oblivion.

When she woke the room was almost dark. Her watch told her that it was nearly half-past four. Heavens, teatime in an English country house, and she might have missed it.

There was no question of missing it. Silver teapots and Worcester porcelain were set out in the Long Drawing Room. Doran noted that the porcelain was twentieth-century Worcester; it would be most regrettable but not tragic if there were a breakage.

To her surprise the tea-drinkers were few. Morven Cair was among them, at a window, gazing into the cheerless landscape as though seeing Sybilline visions. Doran introduced herself and asked why the tea was not more in demand. "Though I suppose I'm very late for it."

"I would not say that." The voice was deepish, the tone measured and tinged with a very, very educated Scots accent, Highland polished in Edinburgh, lulling to the ear. "A lot of them have gone to see the big stuff into the van."

"Van? I'm afraid I'm new to this."

"Well, most of the public bring their offerings personally, but it's not to be expected that they could manage heavy furniture. So we send a removal firm round to pick up anything too big for a car."

"Then we know what's expected?"

"In that line, yes. Owners telephone beforehand."

"Oh. I expect you know all the ropes, Miss Cair?"

A slow, good-humoured smile. "Mrs. I'm a Campbell by birth."

Doran stopped herself by a whisker from blurting out, "Oh dear, then you were on the wrong side in the Forty-five." What a gaffe, to inflict one's personal romantic sentiments about the gallant, doomed Rebellion of Bonnie Prince Charlie on a complete stranger who was probably an impeccable Campbell, and certainly a most beautiful one. There was a sort of irridescence about her, a soft bloom on her skin that rivalled the Worcester tea service and its painted fruit, a shining look to large full eyes—in the left one there was the very slightest of casts, curiously attractive. Her long throat had a slender strength, like a smooth rounded pilaster.

Doran noticed the hands which were pouring another cup of tea, creamy white, small for a woman of her build, with engaging dimples where most people had unengaging knuckles. Hands that would look well modelled as vases in bisque, holding a little flower vase. Rather like pricing objects, the way one sized up women for their attractiveness in relation to one's own, and men for their—attractiveness.

Henry entered. "Ah, tea! How splendid. Well, that's all the carting and heaving done. The hall's being set up like a slave auction."

Doran went out to see. It was indeed transformed. Gone were the country-house homely touches, dogs, whips, boots and outdoor garments waiting for owners who would never return. The easy chairs and small sofas which had been dotted about were gone too.

Instead, the floor space held pieces of furniture and objects—chairs, tables, small bureaux, a huge and hideous vase, big enough to contain one of the Forty Thieves. On the raised gallery that ran along the inner side of the hall were ranged larger pieces, a secretaire bookcase, a dismantled brass bed, a Welsh dresser, a long-case clock. Round these things the experts were moving, peering and discussing. Bert Prinn was hovering tenderly over a collection of glass laid out on a table. He raised a rapt face as Doran passed him. His voice was of the Midlands, loud and rough-edged.

"I had to go myself and fetch this stuff. They just won't wrap them properly, they never learn. They could have damaged *that*."

It was a Jacobite dram glass, hopefully engraved with the white rose of the Stuarts and its two buds. Doran shook her head sadly over the fate of those who had, unlike the Campbells, been on the right side in the Forty-five, and passed on to Howell, who was standing by a chair, with the air of a man defending a besieged stronghold.

The chair was a plain enough side chair, its slip seat in tatters, one of its cabriole legs with an obvious clumsy mend, damage to the splat, and some nasty new varnish disfiguring its crest.

"That's not very nice," Doran said. "Why are you guarding it? Nobody's going to nick it."

Howell threw her a scornful look and muttered something in Welsh, adding, "Where you been, while we was all helpin' out? Lazy you are."

"Well, I felt a bit tired. What a mangy lot of stuff. Is it all going to be like this?"

"How should I know? Won't be too much of it, that's for sure, seein' they'll have to come by car, this dump bein' in the middle of nowhere."

Doran inspected the furniture, as others were doing. A number of people were laying out plain tables for display purposes, providing chairs for the experts and their public, checking supplies of pencils, paper and magnifying glasses. A harassed-looking woman in a boiler suit, Miss Deirdre Pell, was organizing all this, colliding with a spike-haired girl of apparently little more than school age, who turned out to be the anchor-person for the local television station. Four camera-crew members heaved their equipment and cables from place to place, under her instructions, which Doran was surprised to hear crouched in language more suited to a rugger dressing room than a stately home. Well, it was all experience.

It was mid evening before order prevailed and calm set in with the departure of the television crew. In the rest of the house candles had been lit in sconce and candelabrum, with mellowly beautiful effect, discreetly backed up by electricity, and log fires crackled. The dogs had reappeared. One followed Doran into the small, intimate library. When she settled comfortably by the fire with her feet up, he too settled on the rug with his great head on her knees, having cast a hopeful upward look in case there was room for him to curl up on her lap.

She had selected from the shelves a book of ghosts and legends, ravishingly illustrated by Dulac. It seemed the right thing for a winter's night. A maid put her frill-topped head round the door to announce that a buffet supper was available in the dining room. Doran replied that she would be along later.

"Perhaps you'd care for something in here, madam?"

"How very kind. Yes, that would be lovely." She settled for a sandwich and a glass of white wine. This was service indeed. She returned to the illustration she had been lost in, a high room glittering with half-seen colours in heraldic shield and tapestry, veiled in swirling mists, through which a spectral crowned figure was materializing, clad in silver armour.

"What are you reading?" asked a voice, so close that she jumped, sending the book crashing to the floor. The Labrador rolled reproachful eyes.

"Sorry. Didn't mean to alarm you." Dermid Scance stood over her. His gaunt appearance blended in her mind for a moment with the ghostly knight in the picture. What a painfully thin young man, in this house of plenty.

He paused, studying the Dulac picture, before handing it back.

"This. Yes. The skeleton in armour."

"It reminded me more of Keats's *pale Kings and Princes too, pale warriors, death-pale were they all.*"

She knew now that it was of Keats that Dermid reminded her. There was no actual likeness, just a look, and the same proportions and colouring.

Doran was intrigued, sorry for him, remembering Henry's words.

"Sit down. Would you like some supper?" Without waiting for an answer she tugged the embroidered bell-pull by the fireplace. In such a house it should work, and it did, producing within moments another smiling maid, clad in an evening uniform even prettier than the daytime one. Doran ordered more wine and sandwiches. If the poor creature was bent on palely loitering she could at least supply him with something more substantial than roots of relish sweet with honey wild and manna dew: whatever that might be.

"It's very kind of you," he said, "but I don't drink wine, only soft drinks, tonic or something. Oh, and sandwiches which aren't meat or cheese or egg, please."

"Low protein," said the knowledgeable maid, with a knowledgeable nod.

"It's quite extraordinary," Doran said, as they ate (yes, he was hungry) "but I can't get away from Keats at the moment. He keeps coming up all the time. Only yesterday my husband said . . ." She switched direction. "You know how it is when something's mentioned that you haven't thought of for ages, and then you read of it in every newspaper you pick up?"

"Yes. So you don't often think about Keats. Do you know much about him?"

"Only what most people know." In fact, considerably more, but she was curious to discover what knowledge of the poet Scance thought important. Had he ever studied his own reflection? "One of the great Romantics of the early nineteenth century—Regency? Yes. Passionate, sensual—contemporary critics despised him for being lush with his adjectives. Died of consumption, young."

"Aged twenty-six, 1821."

"Right. Madly in love with the girl next door."

"Miss Fanny Brawne."

"Miss Fanny Brawne. Who didn't reciprocate?"

'She did! She wasn't the hard-hearted teaser even his friends thought her. She reciprocated to the extent of becoming engaged to him. It was unconsummated love that helped to kill him, not unrequited love. They lived there in Hampstead in twin houses with only a party wall between them. Imagine it! She was allowed to pay him daily visits, but the stupid bloody conventions didn't allow anything more."

"Or the health regulations, one would imagine."

"No! Nobody knew anything about infection. Keats had caught the thing from nursing his dying brother." Scance took a gulp of tonic. "They sent him to winter in Italy. To Rome, where he died in torment."

"He would. A nasty bug, TB, mercifully stamped out now. And of course Switzerland would have been the place . . ."

"No, you don't understand. The torment was in his mind, that he could never see Fanny again, never possess her. He couldn't even bear to read her letters—they were buried with him. People can die of love, you know."

As he talked, Scance's pale face had developed two bright

spots of colour around the sharp cheekbones, his eyes a dangerous wildness, as though he had the once-dreaded disease, or he were slightly mad. Doran decided to cool the climate of the conversation.

"When I was much younger," she said, "I remember I used to get most terribly involved with people in the past and want quite desperately to be able to go back on a time machine and rescue them, or tell them not to, or whatever. You know, Charles the First being so stubborn that he lost his head for it, martyrs sticking to their guns instead of sensibly recanting, the Light Brigade being ordered to charge: all that. Then one day I realized I was wasting my energies. Those people were dead, nothing could bring them back to life again, and their troubles were over. They'd gone on to something better . . . one hopes," she added hastily. "So I didn't do it any more, or hardly at all. It seems to me"—she stroked the Labrador's ears lengthily—"that you've become totally involved with Keats's troubles, and it's not doing you any good. Didn't he . . ." she tried not to give too much of her knowledge away. "Didn't he write something about being in love with death?"

"I have been half in love with easeful Death."

"Yes, well. No doubt he thought he was, but when it came to the point he didn't care for death at all. Did you know that you can develop false symptoms of diseases by dwelling on them?" She hoped that was true.

"I wouldn't mind," Scance muttered.

"Oh yes you would. There was nothing romantic about pulmonary TB, it was just as disgusting as any other terminal infection. So have that last sandwich, and I'll ring for some more, and don't brood. Keats wouldn't thank you."

Scance was staring at her with something like awe.

"You're very wise. Are you—do you counsel people?"

"Well, I'm a vicar's wife, and I have once or twice dealt

with the odd parishioner raving in the hall. Not often, thank goodness.''

''And you're very beautiful. A vulnerable sort of beauty. Did you say you have a husband?''

''For a vicar's wife it's usual. Actually, I must rush off and telephone him. Why don't you go and join the others, instead of staying here? There'll be plenty left in the dining room. See you later—tomorrow, anyway.''

She left him staring after her with the same mesmerized expression. There, if I mistake not, she thought, is a man suffering not so much from an imaginary disease as from a very real Belle Dame Sans Merci. *Full beautiful, a faery's child.* The dazzling Mrs. Cair.

Her telephone at home was answered after ten rings, and her heart gave a leap at the expectation of Rodney's voice. But it was Carole's, cold and flat as usual.

''Yes, the vicar's in. He's with Helena, been with her most of the evening, had his supper in there. Shall I get him for you?''

For a moment Doran didn't answer. Rodney must have heard the telephone, since there was an extension in the hall and another in Helena's bedroom. He must surely have guessed the call was from her. He had had plenty of time to pick up the telephone by now and interrupt the conversation with Carole. He could have taken the initiative of telephoning the Manor, to make peace about last night and their unloving farewell. Why had he been with Helena all evening? She should have been doing her homework alone, attended on when necessary by Carole.

''No,'' she heard herself saying, in a voice as flat and cold as Carole's own. ''No, don't bother him. I just rang to check that everything's all right.''

'' 's OK. Only Ozzy sent to say he's done his back in and

he can't fetch the wood. And Tybalt's been sick on the lounge carpet.''

"Tybalt shouldn't be in the drawing room, he's a kitchen cat until he's trained.'' (And don't make his name sound like Tibbles, you tiresome girl, even if you think it ought to be.)

"Can I go early tonight? It's ever so dark and slippy.''

"You'll have to ask the vicar about that, won't you. Good night.''

As she slammed down the receiver she knew quite certainly that Carole was saying to herself Rude Cow. Possibly even Rude Old Cow, though there could be no more than three years between them.

Suddenly cold inside, as though she had swallowed ice, Doran went to the dining room. The buffet tables bore a depressing array of empty and, worse, half-empty plates. A young waiter in a tailcoat with brass buttons and a smartly tied cravat still smiled bravely behind a rank of bottles which had been well patronized, judging by the drained glasses scattered about. A few torpid guests remained. Mercia Lang sat alone with the remains of a drink, glancing about her as birds do when they feed on lawns. Doran noticed again the indefinable odd air about her. Pretty but ordinary, any housewife from anywhere, to look at: but something else untypical. Nervous? Undecided? Afraid? Twitchy, certainly, restless hands and feet and a false smile when one caught her eye. All of a twitter, one might say.

Morven Cair reclined on a chaise longue in precisely the attitude of Madame Recamier. She wore a shimmering dress of India muslin, which surely must conceal some thermal undergarment if the lovely creature was indeed human. She was reading, watched darkly and devotedly by Dermid Scance. The half-empty glass beside her seemed to contain tomato juice—not, Doran guessed, a Bloody Mary.

Bert Prinn sat staring unhappily at nothing, and gave Doran an unwelcoming glance as she approached him. She had seen him eyeing the public telephone covetously while she was using it. She sat down beside him.

"Do tell me," she said, "and if you think I'm appallingly inquisitive and rude, say so, because I am—inquisitive, anyway. Howell tells me that your name's actually Ethelbert. Is it really, and if so, why?"

"Yes, it is," Prinn snapped. "I don't know how that got out. It's been made a stupid joke of all my life and I've done what I can to hush it up."

"I can well understand that—I don't blame you, and I won't mention it to anybody. But why? Did your mother want a daughter called Ethel, or had she a passion for Anglo-Saxon history?"

Prinn gave her a withering look as he got to his feet, the sort of look a bull might cast on someone in a scarlet tracksuit sauntering into its field.

"I can't see it matters. And in any case it's got nought to do wi' you. Excuse me, I've got to go and phone."

Doran shook her head at his retreating back. It was always a sign of emotional disturbance when people let their regional accents slip. Unless they made a feature of having a regional accent, as some media figures did all the time.

Falk Lydgate stood before a pier glass beside the central fireplace, hands clasped behind his back, the stance of any viewer in an art gallery. But what was Falk Lydgate viewing? Surely not his own image. No, the room and those in it. Which of them in particular?

"If you want a nightcap, don't have gin," said Henry, behind her. "It'll make you even more depressed."

"How do you know I'm depressed?"

"Your shoulders droop."

"All right, I'm depressed. I don't think I'll have a nightcap at all, I'll go to bed."

"Good idea. It's going to be an early start tomorrow—

41

doors open at nine. But at least it shouldn't be hard going, in a remote spot like this.''

Lydgate left the room just before them. When they passed the telephone cubicle in the inner hall he was there, dialling.

As they went together up the broad staircase Doran longed to pour out to Henry the story of her evening, Dermid Scance's strange outburst, her attempt to reach Rodney, her flat disappointment. It would even have been a comfort to gossip with him about the other experts. Was Scance really love-crazed about Morven Cair, or was it a pose? Could that lady be as enigmatic as she looked? Why was Mercia Lang so nervous? Was Lydgate keeping watch on somebody, and if so, whom? But tomorrow, not now.

At the point where the staircase branched upwards, left and right, she expected Henry to leave her, knowing that his room was on the opposite side to hers. But he stayed beside her. In silence they reached her door.

"Well," she said, "good night, Henry."

He looked down at her quizzically. It was not at all the sort of look with which he had gently dismissed her, that night long ago in Oxford. She knew that he was going to kiss her, and that she would respond with desperate eagerness.

After that they said nothing. Henry touched her cheek gently, and left her. Who had called her wise, that night? It was Henry who was wise.

When she descended the staircase at breakfast time the hall was in chaos, a microcosm of Frith's canvas of Paddington station. The camera crews were rushing about, repositioning their gear, men and maids were running in and out with very un-Victorian disarray. Miss Pell hurtled, wild-eyed, past Doran, almost knocking her over.

Howell appeared, a vision of early morning frowst.

"What on earth's the matter with everybody?" Doran asked him.

He smirked. "Coaches, that's what. Rolling up in coaches, aren't they."

"Are they? Where? Let me see." She elbowed past him to a window. Two huge touring coaches were indeed already parked among numerous private cars in the drive, another one lumbering behind looking for space. Their occupants were pouring out, muffled like Eskimos against the biting cold, and weighted down with containers. Doran saw carrier bags, shopping bags, airline holdalls, boxes and parcels, black plastic dustbin liners. Two men staggered under the weight of a tea chest, a woman carried a large cat basket. All heavy-laden, all eager for judgement and the hope of treasures: and all converging on the front door of the house.

"You see? I told you."

"Yes, I see. It's going to be absolute murder."

And so, a few hours later, it was.

Chapter 4

. . . Their murder'd man

Doran, the roadshow novice, was excited if almost over-powered by the press of folk who crowded round her little table with their offerings.

"My grandfather brought it back from China, oh, about seventy years ago."

"No, we haven't got the pair, it got smashed, the other one."

"Oh, shouldn't we have made it into a lamp? We thought it looked nice, the little lady holding it up like that. Oh, Chelsea, is it?"

"Would these be valuable? Mother always said they were rubbish, but I liked them."

"Oh, my goodness—as much as that?"

There were some nice surprises: an early Derby squirrel, eating a nut with a sly askance look, and only the smallest bit of damage to his tail, a Staffs earthenware jug decorated with figures from pantomime, a delicious fan painted for the Dutch East Indian market. But some ingenious person had touched up the lovely faded tints with modern gilding and clumsy crude colours from a child's paint box. No other fan arrived. A watercolour of roses in a vase, unsigned, looked so promising that Doran asked the bringer to leave it for examination.

She liked the old customers best, the ones who had had the object forty years or more, who would never sell it, however valuable it turned out to be. She was exasperated (though polite) with others who ought to have been able to tell plastic from glass or jade, and Britannia metal from silver. She was short with at least three customers who were quite plainly dealers, there to get a free valuation, or even, in one case, to try her out.

Because she was valuing small objects she was continuously busy. Out of the corner of her eye she saw other experts slipping away for coffee or other purposes, and being temporarily replaced by stand-ins, but nobody offered to stand in for her. Henry had disappeared from his table—not surprising. Who could be bringing his quality of goods to such a modest occasion? Howell was enjoying himself, wearing a smile which matched his tomcat moustache: Doran guessed that he was humming *Dafydd y garreg wen* under his breath. So he had made a killing of some sort—the shabby chair? Lydgate was being frostily pontifical about a country Chippendale table, which he clearly despised deeply, to the owner's chagrin. Dermid was explaining patiently to the old man who had thought the long-case clock a priceless treasure that its movement was considerably more modern than its body, and that frankly it was not worth a great deal. "But nice. Take care of it." Doran decided that he was a very kind young man, if slightly mad.

Prinn was pretending to listen, his gaze wandering (telephone-wards, possibly?) to a woman telling the sort of story punters do tell busy experts.

"My aunt used to go and see this old lady, very good family, she was, used to keeping servants, but of course they'd all left when the war came. She just had the one to look after her and keep the big house clean, a girl from the village. Well, my aunt could see this girl wasn't up to much, because the teacups were all smudged where she hadn't washed them properly, and you could write your name in the dust on the furniture."

Prinn yawned.

"Then one day the old lady said that seeing my aunt had been so kind to her she was going to give her a piece of her collection of Waterford glass. (My aunt liked nice things.) So she went to the cabinet and got the glass out, one piece after another, wine glasses and tumblers and all sorts, and told my aunt to choose something. And my aunt didn't know what to say, because she could see most of them weren't Waterford at all. It turned out that the girl was a Smasher, like so many of them, and that whenever she'd broken a glass washing up she'd replaced it from Woolworth's. And the old lady being short-sighted . . ."

Prinn turned away without an apology to speak to someone else. Oh come, Aethelbert, thought Doran, at least pretend to have a few manners. I don't think I really care for you much. Manners makyth man, you know . . .

The milling television crew had been joined by a roving presenter from Radio Dela, a man with the face of a slightly weary Gothic angel, or Sir Lancelot several years on. Just the age Doran liked. She watched him with interest, and threw him an inviting smile as he turned in her direction. But his attention was distracted by the entrance of Morven, a radiant vision, doubtless refreshed by coffee. With disappointment Doran saw enchantment dawn on his face, as he settled himself and his tape recorder at Morven's table.

It was very unfair. She had known he would be exactly her type, even to the musical voice she could hear in snatches asking the usual questions, a velvet-brown voice, slightly edged. He was telling some story in an assumed Scots accent, very good, which was making Morven laugh, blast her.

One of the young footmen was trying to attract Doran's attention.

"Miss Fairweather—if I could trouble you . . ."

"Of course. What is it?"

"Your car—I believe it's yours, the Volvo estate. Would

46

you mind moving it round the back? One of the coaches has gone and parked badly, and you might get it knocked.''

"All right. But I'll have to get someone to look after my table.'' Howell was temporarily unoccupied. She beckoned to him.

"Can you see to this for a few minutes? I've got to re-park. You look very pleased with yourself.''

"Oh, I am, I am, love.''

"Tell me later.'' She hurried out through the crush of people. The atmosphere was stuffy from the varied odours they all gave off, and the television lights only added to the airless sensation. So that once outside and coatless, she winced as the icy air hit her. The sky was a nasty blend of gunmetal grey and sulphurous yellow. *Numb were the Beadsman's fingers* . . . they'd have been even more numb if the poor old wretch had had to fumble with car keys and a stiff handbag zip and try to start an engine that seemed to have seized up.

At last it started. She manoeuvred Harris past the obstructive coach, round the side of the house, to where other cars, presumably those of staff, were already parked. Yes, there was plenty of space, even for elongated Harris with his uncompromising rear end—like a bustle, which must have been very difficult to cram into some Victorian chairs, and how lucky one was to be able to drive in trousers.

Harris slid obediently into his place. Doran got out, locked the door, and made for what looked like a back entrance which would save her going round the front of the house again.

And fell over a body.

"What the hell's up with you?'' Howell was staring at her, as were others who had seen her frantic rush into the hall. Her teeth were chattering too much to allow speech, but she pulled him towards one of the long windows where fewer people were gathered.

"Right, now what is it? Come on, Doran. You ill or something?"

"There's a—a man. Out there. Dead."

"Here, sit down. What man? How d'you know he's dead?"

"I—know. I touched him, and he was cold." A long shudder shook her. "Not like—any other sort of cold."

"*Duw!* Who is it?"

"I don't know. Just a man. Never seen him before. I've—never seen anyone dead before, come to that. Yes I have, of course, my parents. But that was different." She laughed, the laugh threatening to continue. Howell gave her a sharp shake.

"None of that. You come along with me." He propelled her through the crowd, who made way for them, staring at her white face. Somehow they were in the dining room, by the fire, and she was being plied with brandy and scalding hot coffee. Other people were there, two maids and Miss Pell. Howell masterfully waved them back. He spoke crisply to Miss Pell, who looked terrified, nodded, and vanished.

Doran, somewhat better, smiled weakly up at him. "Thanks, Howell. You're marvellous. Like Britain, best in a crisis."

"And thank *you*, cheeky cow. Drink that coffee up and don't gab."

Drinking it, she began to return to normal, and to be aware that other people had filtered in from the hall. There was the lovely concerned face of Morven Cair, the anxious one of Bert Prinn (who was most unwisely carrying a handsome old Bristol cruet bottle)—the worried baby-doll face of Mercia Lang. Mercia approached Doran, creeping up like a terrified kitten. "The—the man. What—was he like? I don't mean to

48

be morbid, I just wondered . . . he might be somebody I knew . . .''

Doran said, "I can't tell you. I haven't taken it all in yet."

"Did he—have a beard?"

"No, he didn't."

How kind of everyone, and what a fool she felt for attracting such attention. But not, it seemed, Henry's.

Miss Pell returned. "It's all right. Would you please go back into the hall, everyone—except Miss Fairweather, of course. I've told them that she had a nasty fall in the car park and is getting over the shock. Nobody's to say anything at all about—what really happened. We don't want a panic, it would ruin the day. Okay?"

Murmuring, with backward glances at Doran, they left, but for Howell.

"You'd better go too," she told him. "I'm perfectly all right—at least I will be in a minute."

"If you say. I'll fend off the wolves."

Left alone, her thoughts went back to the moment when she had hurried between two parked cars and gone sprawling. Picking herself up, shaken, she looked down at what had tripped her. He was a smallish man, middle-aged, dark hair—what there was of it—wearing a brown roll-neck chainstore sweater and dark trousers. His appearance was remarkable only for being ordinary; it was a face easily forgotten, unless seen as it was now, shocked and still, the eyes staring and the mouth open.

He had fallen forwards, his head turned slightly against the gravel. Doran bent and heaved him on to his back, as well as she could with the two cars crowding her in. No rigor mortis, so he hadn't been dead long. Couldn't have been, anyway, with so many people about. The hand she touched reluctantly was clammily cold, the palm scratched where it had come into contact with the ground.

Something, the instinct she trusted, was telling her that

this was no mere accidental death, but what her friend Constable Sam Eastry would call suspicious circumstances. The face was not the colour she associated with heart attacks, but it was undoubtedly a nasty, unhealthy colour. (Well, it would be.) No sign of outward injury, and a fall from no distance at all, merely the man's own height, could not have killed.

Sam had told her that in suspicious circumstances one must not move the body or do anything to erase fingerprints or footmarks. Simply report the death and call the authorities. She set off for the house, and at that point trembling shock set in.

Now it had subsided, the natural inquisitiveness which had got her into trouble before was upon her. But for the moment her duty lay with the customers in the hall.

They were waiting at her table, also inquisitive.

"All right now, dear?"

"Nasty things, tumbles. I tripped over a paving stone myself, and believe me I was in hospital for three days. . . ."

"Hot sweet tea, that's what you need, if they haven't given you any. . . ."

Doran smiled, said she was fine now, and what had they got to show her? She was rewarded by an attractive and an obviously genuine Henriette Ronner ink drawing of cat with kittens, and a quite rare Goss commemorative of the opening of the Crystal Palace.

Someone's hand was warm on her shoulder. *Not* an over-affectionate punter, but Henry. At last. "I heard about it. Sorry I wasn't there to support you—a man had an object he thought was a Greek statue in the boot of his car and insisted on my going out to see it. Not Greek, in fact, 1930s cinema décor. Are you really all right?"

"Henry, if anyone else asks me that I shall shriek. Yes, I am, and what did you hear?"

"What happened. From Howell. He seemed to think I

ought to know. There's going to be a lunch break in five minutes—let's eat together.''

"Why not?" The public dispersed to collect packed lunches from cars, or eat snacks in a Victorian conservatory given over to refreshments. In the dining room a few staying hotel guests mingled with experts for soup, slices of quiche, turkey mousse and rather good hamburgers. Rodney would have said something ingenious about funeral baked meats: Doran dismissed the image of Rodney.

Long-skirted girls in their 1890 aprons waited, poured, chatted and smiled continuously. "What an extremely decorative lot they are," Henry reflected. "Domestics have changed a lot, remembering old *Punch* cartoons, sluttish downtrodden slavies.''

"These aren't domestics. They're somebody's debby daughters, filling in between acting jobs, or young housewives earning an honest penny. *Belle du Jour* stuff.''

"Mm. I seem to remember that *la Belle* in that film was a daytime prostitute.''

"Well, whatever. Never mind." At that moment one of the waitresses stepped on the hem of her skirt and crashed to the floor, bringing a bottle and two plates with her. What she said raised Henry's eyebrows.

"You may be right," he said. "Or ingénues have changed—how should I know, buried in my dusty antiquities as I am?''

"How indeed, not that I believe you are. What did Howell tell you?''

"About the corpse in the car park. Just that. A title for a thriller; not a very good one, perhaps.''

"No, very ordinary. Ornery, though that means something else in American, doesn't it?" The corpse had been ordinary, not a person to arouse murderous anger, or an obvious villain, by the look of him. And yet Doran still felt that there was something very wrong. It would have been a relief to discuss it with Henry, nice Henry. But he knew nothing of her previous experiences of crime, and somehow it was not the moment to disclose them. This time she was on her own, with no Rodney to listen and help and defend, if need be.

She became aware, quite quickly, that others knew about the fatality. Of course they would. Through the windows of the dining room a police car could be seen winking its blue light, the white bulk of an ambulance beyond it. The public must know by now, and indeed heads were appearing round the door in quest of information.

Lydgate was looming over her. "I believe you've had an unpleasant experience."

"Well, yes, rather."

Scance was behind him. "Morven told me about it." And trust you to drag in her name, for the pleasure of saying it, thought Doran. She fielded questions, unwillingly. Henry said in her ear, "You'll get nothing to eat. Come on, we'll go somewhere quiet." But as they prepared to leave with their plates and glasses the grandest of the young cravated footmen was catching her eye and politely beckoning.

"The police would like a word, Miss Fairweather."

In a small room off the main kitchen area waited two men who could not possibly have been anything but CID. Indeed, Doran recognized the senior one, by whom she had been interviewed a few months before after the arrest of the antiques thief and murderer, Tony Taddeus.

"Inspector Burnelle. How nice. Though I shouldn't say that in the circumstances, I suppose."

"Nice to see you, Miss Fairweather. Though I understand it's not Miss any more."

"No, it isn't, that's just my professional name." Tea, obviously fresh-brewed, had already been supplied in cups vastly more elegant than those of Eastgate nick; the young sergeant, a bulky man, was handling his as though it were literally made of eggshells. Doran continued to refresh herself with the food and wine she had brought through with her.

Burnelle beamed paternally over the huge nylon fur collar of the army surplus coat he was still wearing. "Police interrogation holds no terrors for you, I can see that."

"Far from it. Some of my happiest memories are of you gentlemen—particularly last year. And I *have* been wondering about this—the man I fell over."

"You didn't recognize him?"

"Never set eyes on him."

"Nor have any of the people we've questioned—or rather the people who've questioned us, because a lot seem to have got to know about it, somehow. Nobody's missing a companion or member of a coach party. Seems he arrived alone."

"In his own car. You've found the car?"

"Not yet. My sarge—Steve here—is just going out to re-check on parked cars and their owners before we start on the coach parties. I take it not many of the public will have left?"

"I'll be most surprised if they have. They come for a day out, and a day out's what they intend to have. The hall's been getting hotter and hotter and fuller and fuller all morning."

"You didn't see anyone leaving as you re-parked?"

"Not a soul. Some more had just arrived, hence the problem about the badly parked coach. And I could have seen a car going away, in open country like this—right down to the entrance gate. Far from leaving, I think you'll find they're ringing up friends and relations, telling them to hurry up and join the happy throng—*Come, ye thankful people, come*—sorry, we tend to get hymns on the brain at home."

Burnelle stirred his tea, shaking his head. "You're very cynical for a clergyman's lady."

"Not at all, far from it. I just know about the lure of roadshows and sudden deaths. *Was* it sudden, by the way? What does the police surgeon say?"

Behind the inspector's genial regard a shutter came down. "He's only had time to make a superficial examination yet, of course. We shall know more after the p.m."

"You may, I shan't, and I'm interested. He didn't look like a heart case to me. And when I half turned him over I couldn't see any marks on his head, which would have been there if he'd hit it violently. Now what else could cause a man to fall dead in a car park? All right, I don't really expect an answer. Will you be questioning everybody—all my colleagues, for instance?"

"In that case we should have to question everybody in the house. It would take a long time and almost certainly get us nowhere, in what's almost certainly a simple case of cardiac failure. I merely asked you because you discovered the body. I don't think there's anything else you can usefully tell us."

Meaning I can go, and good riddance to me. Aloud, casually, she asked, "By the way, who was he?"

"I'm afraid we can't say, as yet."

"Can't, or won't?"

Burnelle's expression struggled between exasperation and amusement. "When we need recruits for the CID I must remember you, Miss Fairweather. All right, can't. There were no papers on him, nothing in his pockets but coins, a handkerchief, some loose tissues and a comb."

"How curious. He travelled lightly who travelled alone . . . Even more curious that he wasn't wearing a coat, on a day like this."

Burnelle looked pointedly at his watch. Doran drained her wine glass, gathered it up and her plate.

"Well, I mustn't hold you up. Goodbye, Inspector. Good luck with your investigation." She gave him a seraphic smile and left.

The sound of voices drew her to pause at an open door near the back entrance by which she had rushed into the house after her discovery. It was clearly the flower room, empty vases stacked by a sink, dead flowers heaped in a bin, something else dead being removed on a stretcher, covered with a sheet, by the police sergeant and three young footmen: the poor anonymous man who had left the world without a farewell, without any means of identification; without even an overcoat. Rodney would have said a small prayer for him, unobtrusively. Doran did so, for Rodney's sake as well as the corpse's.

She felt a very strong impulse to telephone Rodney, who should at that moment be having lunch made and served by Carole. On her way upstairs to her bedroom telephone she changed her mind.

The number she dialled, when the switchboard gave her, with courteous swiftness, an outside line, was that of the Abbotsbourne community constable, Sam Eastry. They were old friends, and associates in more than one criminal case. Sam, who had lost a beloved young daughter, looked on Doran somewhat as a replacement who might be grown up but was still in need of care and protection, and occasionally of unofficial help.

The voice of Sam's wife Lydia informed her that Sam had nearly finished his dinner and was on his way to the telephone. "When he heard it was you," said Lydia, resigned to her husband's impending involvement in yet another strange case featuring antiques.

Sam's deep warm voice, with its slight Kentish accent, took over.

"Doran. What can I do for you?"

"Something a bit off the cuff, I'm afraid. Listen." She gave him, with crisp economy, a summary of the events of the morning. "They've taken him—whoever he was—off to the nearest mortuary, I suppose. Do you know which one it would be? Good. Well, can you somehow find out the result of the p.m.? I know it's got nothing to do with you. But there must be ways—someone you know who wouldn't mind letting a word drop."

Sam exhaled not so much a sigh as a deep, patient breath.

"There's a chap that assists the pathologist at Barminster. I expect he could pull a string or two, for the price of a pint, next time I see him."

"I'll stand you that, don't worry—treble Scotch, if you like. I just need to know what this corpse died of. They might find a stab wound, or signs of an injection, or—oh, anything. If it was heart failure, then I'm wrong, because I don't think it was."

"Why?"

"Because, mainly, he wasn't wearing a topcoat, on a morning when everybody else is wearing everything from anoraks and lodens to grannie's rabbit. If he'd just got out of his car, he'd have worn it into the house, surely. If he'd just come out of the house to go back to his car, he'd have put it on again—unless he was superhumanly resistant to cold temperatures."

Sam sighed, or breathed heavily, again. "It sounds dicey to me, Doran. There might have been a dozen reasons why he didn't bother to wear a coat. A chap I knew used to walk across the top of the North Downs every Christmas, in just a windcheater."

"I note you say 'used to.' "

"Well, he's dead, as a matter of fact. Pure coincidence—"

'Right. There's also the fact that the corpse hadn't any means of identification in his pockets. No papers, driving licence, credit cards, no nothing."

"They could have been in the pockets of his coat."

"Locked in his car (and by the way, what about his car keys?) Or hanging on a peg in the house?"

"You're theorizing."

"I'm reasoning. I live with a man, remember? I know their habits."

"What are you trying to prove?"

"Nothing. I hope I'm not keeping you from your pudding, or coffee, or whatever? Good. I simply have a feeling that he knew somebody in the manor house, and I'd like to find out who it was."

"A funny lot, are they, your experts?" Sam asked. He had a low opinion of Doran's dealer friends in Eastgate, particularly Howell Evans.

"Not in the least funny. I wouldn't trust all of them with my life or my purse, but on the whole they seem fairly stainless. I just want to know. Sorry to land you with this. Oh, and you will find out from your people when Burnelle's boys come across the car, won't you—that ought to be easier than the autopsy."

"Yes, much," said Sam heavily. He hung up, and returned to the ginger pudding of which he was particularly fond; it had gone cold, and Lydia was a shade more irritable than usual about it. Some men in his position would have brushed Doran off for a meddling member of the public, but he knew her well, and the—could you call it psychic?—intuition of which she was at times capable. No, psychic was not the word. He, also, a student of literary criminology, knew the rules of the Detection Club, which specifically banned feminine intuition and the supernatural. He was not sure what to call Doran's flair for finding something wrong in an apparently innocent situation. If he had accepted promotion in the force, instead of sticking in his precious little patch, Abbotsbourne, he would doubtless have known more about such things.

Returning to the hall, Doran found the Roadshow in full swing again. As she had guessed, everybody now knew about the fatality and nobody had let it make the slightest difference to their enjoyment of the day. A man was dead. Well, it must have been quick and painless, poor soul, from what they said. And any of the new arrivals might be carrying almost priceless treasure in a plastic bag, for any one of these sharp-eyed demigods to detect. Then they would say Oooh, I never gave it a thought, how much it might be worth. No, of course I wouldn't sell it, not after it's been in the family so long. But they would, as soon as they got it home.

Again she was a target for eyes. She felt unspoken questions coming at her. "What did the police say? Do they know anything yet? Is the body still there?" One woman actually asked this last question. Doran answered, "No idea," and put on a pair of spectacles with plain lenses which she kept by her as a morale-booster.

Everything went out of her mind except the job in hand. She inspected and priced ugly objects which were yet reasonably commercial, potentially valuable objects shockingly restored by unskilled hands, or not restored at all ("It got broken and some of the pieces never got put back, but it was so pretty I kept it"), horrible contemporary kitsch and kitsch of some thirty or forty years ago, equally horrible but now saleable in the right place at the right time.

And some nice pieces, pieces which justified the whole: an enchanting baby doll wearing most of its original clothes, a Royal Doulton figurine of a crinolined pink-cheeked simpering miss, very like Mercia Lang, a Clarice Cliff vase, a Victorian papier-mâché tea caddy with mother-of-pearl flowers.

Some of the punters talked far too much, some just wanted to listen. She began to tell one eager woman how she knew approximately the age of any object.

"It's like knowing, or guessing, the age of anything—a person, for instance. A man or woman of fifty is quite different from someone of twenty-five, and not only in physical condition. One can't really mistake a Victorian piece for a Georgian one, because the Victorians thought quite differently about style, shape and decoration. To them, Georgian simplicity was plain and ugly, whereas to the twenties of this century Victorian stuff was heavy and fussy and only fit to be thrown out. Then there was a reaction . . .''

A hush round her made her look up. Not only were the public gathered round her table, gogglingly intent on this free lecture, but the young television director had a camera trained on her and the other experts had paused to listen. Lydgate sneered, Howell's face was all cheerful derision and only Henry's look was kindly.

Doran blushed violently and stopped in mid sentence. Fortunately somebody had just opened up a parcel, giving her an excuse for turning to inspect the contents.

Over cups of tea, later in the afternoon, she said to Henry, ''I felt absolutely awful when I realized everyone was listening. I'm sorry, I made a fool of myself.''

''Rubbish. It was just what they wanted to hear, what they came for.''

''Pretty elementary, that stuff, gal,'' said Howell. ''Anyway, they all know it themselves by now.''

Lydgate said nothing. Morven bestowed a slow, lovely half-smile, like the Mona Lisa faintly amused by Leonardo's attempt at a rude story. Dermid Scance was looking at the smiling mouth: Doran was sure he had not heard a word of her own impromptu lecture.

Henry seldom looked at Morven. Possibly he was embarrassed by Dermid's infatuation, or completely immune to her charms since his own rejected addresses.

By the time tea had been drunk all the lights were on, in addition to the desk lamps which illuminated the tables. Doran glanced out of a window. The sky was darkening— not that there was scope for it to grow much murkier or more lurid than it had been all day. In the hot room draughts were beginning to make themselves felt.

The public were leaving, in ones and twos, murmuring about lighting-up time. The experts, weary and dry-throated by now, began to hope for release. At five o'clock the Roadshow organizer took the centre of the room and made a nice little speech. By half-past the public had left, the last car tail lights had vanished down the drive. Footmen and maids were unobtrusively clearing up the room. The experts thankfully retired.

Doran, air-starved, stood on the front steps and breathed deeply. The air, though welcome, was intensely cold, as intense as the darkness had now become, country dark with no light showing. Very nonsensically, it seemed as though it had begun inside the room and spread outside. . . . *And there was a darkness over all the earth until the ninth hour.* That was what Rodney would have thought of, the Great Darkness. She longed so much for Rodney that she came very near to going to her car, coatless as she was, like the dead man, and driving straight home.

A few flakes of snow began to fall. Then more, and heavier.

Some two hours later the experts, bathed, changed and more or less restored to themselves, gathered for drinks in the inner hall. They chattered of their finds and their nonfinds. Morven had found a Coalbrookdale basket with only slight damage, Prinn an eighteenth-century English wine bottle, as well as the Jacobite dram glass. Lydgate seemed to have found nothing worth talking about.

Doran sought out Howell, who was gulping lager.

"You look pleased with yourself. Too pleased. What was with that chair you were guarding yesterday, from the minute it came in?"

Howell tried to look as if he failed to remember any chair.

"Oh, *that* chair. Yes, well, it was American, see. The guy's great-grandpa or some such brought it over, after they had that war of theirs. Philadelphia, 1780s."

Doran knew well the strength of the market for American furniture.

"It was a bit plain. And in a very poor state, wasn't it?"

"Nothing that can't be put right. And he's got three more at home, all better than that." He smirked.

"So?"

"I did a deal, didn't I."

"We're buying them ourselves?"

"Yeh. Willie's picking 'em up tomorrow." Willie was their excellent furniture restorer. "He'll do wonders for them little beauties."

"I see. What did you pay the seller?"

Howell told her. It was less than half what he would get from their contact who specialized in the export of American furniture.

She left him without comment. There was no comment one could usefully make on Howell's methods. By the fireplace Henry was examining a carved Romayne panel. His face lit up when he saw her.

"Come and talk to me. What did you find?"

"Nothing sensational, just what I expected—but I made at least one old lady very happy. What did *you* find?"

"Only this." Henry took something out of his pocket and displayed it on his open palm. It lay there, glittering and gleaming in the candlelight. Somebody—who?—gasped.

Then they all gathered, like sheep at a feeding trough, and stared at what Henry had found.

Chapter 5

A casement ope at night

"Oh, it's pretty," said Mercia. "It would look lovely on a chain, except that it's the wrong way up—the face, I mean."

"I think it's meant to be worn as a brooch, actually," said Henry, "longways on. There ought to be a stem or pin projecting from it, but there isn't. Or it could be a pointer to help the reading of a manuscript."

Doran stared, fascinated, at the tiny oval miniature of brilliant-coloured enamel, set deeply in gold round which was a raised inscription. The base of the heart-shape sprang from a golden beast's head—a boar's, perhaps, holding in its mouth what could have been a cup or the top of a socket.

"It looks like a museum piece," she said.

"It *is* a museum piece. At least, a copy of one. The original's in the Ashmolean. Don't you remember it? The Alfred Jewel." He informed the company, "Doran and I were talking about our Oxford days, only yesterday."

"Intriguing," said Lydgate. "One would hardly have thought you were up in the same year."

"We weren't!" Doran snapped. "We just met in Oxford, in—in another way, nothing to do with university."

"Ah." He made it sound as though the other way must have been extremely disreputable.

Morven stretched out a hand. "May I hold it?" Dermid was at her side in an instant, one hand enclosing hers that cupped the jewel. "But it's exquisite," he breathed, and

Doran knew that he meant the fair dimpled hand as much as what it held.

Doran couldn't honestly swear that she remembered the Alfred Jewel, but then she had been totally absorbed in Henry at the time. "Why," she asked him, "would anyone bother to make a copy of it?"

"Museums do, for sale, and a lot of people buy them. You can buy a good mock-up of one of the Elgin Marbles if you want one. I've got a little model of the Venus of Verulamium which was too charming to resist, though I don't make a habit of displaying fakes. I told the man who brought this, gently but firmly, that it was only worth whatever the museum charged, and of absolutely no antique value at all, but the poor chap begged me to keep it overnight and look at it carefully, and he'd come back tomorrow. Hard up, I suppose."

Doran took it from Morven. "What's the inscription? My eyes are fogged up with peering at makers' marks."

"Alfred had me made," said Henry. "In Anglo-Saxon, of course. It really was made for him, they think."

"Was that Alfred the Great?" asked Mercia.

"It was. Good title for him, in fact, not as inapt as Bluff King Hal or Good King Charles—a great soldier and a great scholar, particularly as early as that, ninth century AD Terrific fellow."

Doran was scuffling through her shoulder-bag. "My glass. Where's my glass? Don't say I've lost it."

"Have mine," Bert Prinn offered.

"Thanks, no, mine's a linen prover that magnifies four times. Oh good, it's here."

"Why take the trouble?" sneered Lydgate.

"Why not? Some of us have a well-developed sense of curiosity, even if you haven't." It was not her style to be rude to colleagues, but he had asked for it. She scanned the jewel slowly through her powerful lens. It was certainly cloisonné enamel, not any form of plastic, and, unless her eyes and

63

fingertips misled her, it was certainly set in gold. Expensive form of reproduction, even for a top museum. Celtic, she would have said at a venture, if it had been an original. The colours were very clear and beautiful, the portrait showing a half-length figure wearing something turquoise-coloured and carrying what seemed to be a rose stem. Its hair, or the circlet above the face, was ash-blond.

"What a pretty face," she said, "for the ninth century."

Henry laughed. "Alfred wouldn't thank you, he was all man, and there's his beard to prove it."

"But he hasn't got a beard."

Morven took the jewel back, and Doran's glass. "Certainly no beard there. And what did you say was the inscription, Henry?"

"Alfred had me made."

"Ah. Well, This one says *aelhswith mec heht gewyrcan.* Which I'd interpret as meaning that a woman named Aelhswith had it, or ordered or commanded it, to be made for her. Aelhswith would be modernized as Alice or Alicia. It was the name of Alfred's wife."

Lydgate broke the silence. "It appears you're a specialist in the Anglo-Saxon tongue as well as in all your other—sidelines, Mrs. Cair."

"Naturally," replied the calm, assured voice of Edinburgh, the Athens of the North.

They had all forgotten about their drinks. Now empty and half-empty glasses were snatched up, drained, refilled, as though some sort of unproposed toast were being drunk. To what, Doran wondered? A clever fake or a mind-boggling discovery, a Saxon royal jewel of extraordinary beauty and exquisite workmanship? Henry's expensive spectacles couldn't be all that good, if he'd missed the absence of a beard. When had she and somebody else been talking about Saxon jewellery? Of course—Helena, the other night, showing off about it and saying that a school party was going to see the hoard at Barminster Museum. What a strange thing. And Prinn and Mercia both having Saxon names. It was something in the air, must be.

Howell had not forgotten about his drink. It was still with him, on the mantelpiece between a vase which was not quite Imari and a brass candlestick. He had not contributed a word to the discussion, or come forward to inspect the problem piece. When a Benares gong summoned the company in to dinner he finished his lager, wiped his moustache, and went into the dining room alone. Doran wondered whether he could be, in his odd way, jealous of Henry.

By tacit consent Doran and Henry sat alone at a table away from the centre of the room. Prinn and Mercia were together, showing each other snapshots of their several children. Miss Pell and a man who seemed to be high up in the hotel's hierarchy were sitting talking earnestly with Morven. To-night she wore another Indian dress, of deep crimson, spangled with sequins and flowers embroidered in gold and silver thread, a princess from a Persian painted miniature. Doran, who had been rather pleased with her best winter dress, of the medieval simplicity which was her style, in purple angora-type wool discreetly flecked with a gilt thread, felt out-classed. But fair enough, by such a matchless beauty.

She broached her broccoli timbale starter. Henry was drinking artichoke soup, which he did with a natural grace and poise not invariable in soup-drinkers. No drop of it would venture to spoil his discreet pure silk tie of pearl grey. He was nice to look at in any circumstances.

"Well, well, well," he said, deftly finishing the soup. "Alice's Adventures in the Ashmolean."

"Or, Through the Magnifying Glass."

"Or, Anglo-Saxon Attitudes."

"Precisely." It was a game she had never played with anyone but Rodney: or thought to play. "What will you do with—Alice?"

65

"Just what the man said. Keep her overnight and think about her."

"Who was this man? Did he say where he'd got the jewel, what its provenance was?"

"No, he didn't. He seemed to be in a bit of a hurry to get away."

"I'm not surprised, if it was hot. What was his name?"

"You'll think me terribly naïf, but I didn't ask him."

"Can I look at her again?"

"Not now. I've left her in my room."

"In a drawer from which, when you next go upstairs, she will be missing, purloined by some criminal lurking amongst us. It always happens when you leave valuables in your hotel room, according to the literature I read."

Henry ordered a bottle of St. Emilion to go with the entre-côte farci they were both having; Doran normally disliked eating friendly cows, but felt that her constitution needed building up.

"What," she asked, "do you think about this find, now, without another look at it? If by any chance it *were* missing from your dressing-table drawer, would it be the loss of a nice decorative wrong 'un or a priceless treasure?"

"I don't know, honestly. I might talk to Lydgate about it, later, when he's finished the meal he appears to be enjoying."

Doran glanced across the room. Lydgate was actually smiling, and chatting animatedly with his companion, whose back was towards her. But she recognized the back all too well: it was Howell's. She opened her mouth to make an outrageous comment, then shut it again. No stopping Howell, her pal, down the river.

Instead she asked, "What was he like, this man who brought the jewel in?"

"Like? I really can't tell you. Just an ordinary man—not

in the least memorable. I don't notice other men much, I fear.''

"He must have been like *something*. Tall or short? Dark, fair, grizzled?"

"Oh, dear. Sort of middling height—shorter than me, anyway. Hair colour—I haven't the least idea. But young rather than old, certainly—in the thirties, I should hazard.''

"You're a rotten witness. Voice? Local, regional, cut-glass?"

"Well. Regional, I suppose, if anything, but I couldn't say what region.''

'' 'Enry 'Iggins would have bloody well known.'' Doran saw with gratification that this other professorial Henry took the reference. He was turning out to be almost frighteningly her type.

"So,'' she said, "this man who looks like a bit player in an old film, the sort whose name one can never remember, and who sounds like the same bit player trying out some nebulous accent, was in possession of something which, whatever it is, must be remarkable, one way or another. I find it very odd, that ordinariness of his.''

"Why shouldn't he have been ordinary?''

"The other man was ordinary, too, the dead man in the car park. Quite a crowd of them gathering. *Ceorls*, rather than *twihyndes*, wouldn't you say? And hopefully not up to any *nidings*, but you never know these days.''

Henry laid down his fork. "Doran, you are, without exception, the biggest show-off I ever met. Why don't you and Morven have a public contest of wits, so that we can all decide which of you is the more erudite?''

"Because everybody would be looking at her, not me, and they wouldn't hear a word I said.''

"Not true. I would be looking at you. I'd like to look at you for a very, very long time.''

The hot delicious zabaglione pudding which had been

placed before them was disgracefully cooling in its dishes, the fragrance of mingled brandy and Marsala drifting between them like incense. They were gazing into each other's eyes in that old, old fashion which has led to more entanglements than anything in the history of the world. Doran tasted the pudding's congealing sweetness and said deliberately, *"Lucent syrops, tinct with cinnamon."*

"I'm sorry?"

Thank heaven, he hadn't got that one; he was not infallible.

"The midnight feast Porphyro brought to Madeline's bedside on St. Agnes's Eve. Keats," she explained kindly.

"Thank you. I'll look it up. What happened after the feast?"

Perhaps it had been unwise to mention bedsides. "Shall we have our coffee in the library?" she suggested. "I like it in there." And very possibly the infatuated Dermid Scance would come and interrupt them, which might be a good thing.

But she must first telephone home.

This time it was Helena who answered. "Oh, it's you."

"Yes, it's me, who else? Can I speak to your father, please?"

"It's Daddy's hospital night." Helena's voice was creamy with satisfaction.

"Oh, of course, I'd forgotten." Once a fortnight Rodney took his turn among other clergymen to visit Eastgate Hospital and go on a round of the wards, bestowing comfort, advice and what help he could. Invariably he came back depressed, weighed down with other people's suffering. "*Flit on, cheering angel*, I *don't* think. How did Miss Nightingale do it, among all that stench and blood? It's bad enough now, even with hygiene and everything."

"It was her job," Doran reminded him.

"It's my job too. But I wish it wasn't."

Tonight, Helena said, he had gone out half an hour early,

at six o'clock. "Because of the snow. I hope he'll be all right, driving back. It's getting worse."

"Snow? There were some flakes falling last time I looked out, but . . ."

"Well, if you look out now you'll see there's buckets of it falling. But I expect you've been too busy enjoying yourself to notice."

This was so true that Doran had no reply to it. She told herself that one couldn't even see what was happening outside in rooms so thoroughly and richly curtained, great fires constantly fuelled, candles and electricity lighting every corner.

"Did he leave any message for me?" she asked.

"No, nothing. As a matter of fact, he's hardly mentioned you since you went yesterday morning." As Helena paused to allow this poisoned dart to sink in, Doran was horrified to find a sob choking her throat.

"I don't think it's very kind of you to tell me that," she managed to say, without disgracing herself.

"Well, it's true. Ask Carole if you don't believe me."

"I shouldn't dream of asking Carole." She swallowed. "I hope one of you will be waiting up for him when he gets home. He'll want a hot drink and—and someone to talk to." And much good will he get from either of you young bitches, she thought savagely, listening to Helena's prim assurance that she knew all about that.

Doran was trembling when she put back the receiver. She turned to find Bert Prinn at her side, and struggled to control herself.

"Sorry, have I kept you waiting for the phone?"

"No, no, it's all right. No bloody phone in the room they've given me, mean lot. So long as I get through before too long . . . not but what it's the same time in Northampton as it is here, not like, er . . ."

"Foreign parts?"

"What? Oh, yes." He seemed tongue-tied, or perhaps he was as stupid as he looked. Who in Northampton or anywhere else could possibly want to hear from him?

She went to the ground-floor Ladies, which was fortunately unoccupied, and there with the door locked let herself cry for long enough to relieve the weight on her heart.

Recovered, she pulled aside the pink velvet curtain. Outside was a white world. What had been the lawns and trees at the rear of the house were invisible. Great flakes were falling steadily as though some colossal sheep-shearing were taking place in heaven.

When she joined Henry in the library, her makeup restored, she knew that he was instantly aware of her state. Perhaps he have even anticipated it, for on a small side table along with the coffee cups were two enormous balloon glasses.

"Courvoisier," said Henry. "It seemed a good follow-up to the zabaglione." He had risen at her entrance from a comfortable-looking double-seater sofa of brown buttoned leather which had been put slantwise to the fire. She sank on to it; Henry joined her. The Labrador was present again, accompanied by its sister. This was their evening place, where only thoughtful humans came, who would not be too restless.

The two animals raised their great heads with canine smiles, then settled down again.

"Put your feet up," Henry invited.

"On a dog?"

"Why not?"

Doran experimentally placed them, ankles crossed, on the solid torso of the brother. He gave a soft groan of pleasure. She kicked her shoes off and replaced the feet, clad in her best Dior tights of subtle lavender. She couldn't help knowing that she had pretty feet.

70

Henry regarded them. "Gossamer. Fairies' feet look just like that."

"Do they? Good. Actually, I haven't seen a fairy since I was a little girl. I wonder where the poor things are tonight, in this snow? Do you suppose they burrow into compost heaps like hedgehogs?"

"One would prefer to think not. I rather hope they vanish into underground kingdoms organized by Oberon. Central-heated, of course."

"Do you think Oberon was all that good an organizer? His idea about the little purple flower's juice sorting out the Athenian lovers' mix-up was good, but he doesn't seem to have summed up his staff very well. Puck, for instance. Too flighty—in every sense."

Henry sipped his Courvoisier. "Were you brought up on the works of Shakespeare? Entirely, I mean, without bothering about those of Enid Blyton or whoever it was in your day?"

"Pretty well. The Oxford Playhouse was all done up and re-opened when I was about four, and then there was the new-issue OUDS. People were always doing Shakespeare in college gardens. Now I suppose it's Pinter and Orton." She sighed. The Labrador glanced up sympathetically.

Henry refilled her coffee cup, their hands touching as he passed it to her.

"I'm glad you believe in fairies," she said. "Do you also believe in ghosts?"

They discussed ghosts, at length. The silvery chime of a long-case clock sounded the half-hour. Half-past eleven. "This conversation," Doran said dreamily, "is exactly like one in Noël Coward. *Private Lives*, that's it. They talk about how flat Norfolk is. . . ."

"But really that's not what the conversation's about."

"True. I have to admit that."

A silence fell, during which their eyes were locked. Doran

broke it. "Is Alice still in your dressing-table drawer, or has she vanished, as I predicted?"

"She's still there. Do you want to see her again?"

"Yes."

The house was very still as they went upstairs. The weary experts must have retired; it was interesting to speculate into what bedrooms. Was Morven chastely alone, Doran wondered, or had Dermid had his passionate way and passed that portal? Was Mrs. Mercia Lang still true to her absent husband, or had Bert Prinn found consolation for whoever he was missing in Northampton? As for Howell, in his room over the old stables, it was better not to hazard a guess. Though surely he and old Lydgate wouldn't be . . .

Henry was in the Holbein Room. It was furnished, naturally, on a Tudor theme, with a massive carved four-poster which was a little late for the period but must be worth a small fortune. Doran looked round for pussy-cat pieces, Victorian oak furniture mocking-up the genuine Tudor, but could only see one, a chair. Everything else was either unquestionably right or frankly modern and functional.

On one wall modern portraits (oils on wood, not bad) of Anne Boleyn and Jane Seymour looked away from each other, Anne darkly sultry, Jane appearing, as usual, to be carved out of Gruyère.

"What an unfortunate juxtaposition," she enunciated carefully. "How they must fight when they come out of their frames at midnight. It's almost that now, perhaps we shall see them—what fun. How's your wife, by the way?"

"Very well," Henry replied evenly. "She remarried about four years ago. They live in Paris, I dine with them occasionally."

"How civilized. But then you are so civilized, Henry, that's the thing—one of the things—I like about you." Others were the silvery hair which suited him so well, contrasting with the sun-browned forehead and noble dark brows. Why did grey hair almost always improve men, but seldom women? Some biological reason, no doubt.

"Perhaps not so civilized as you might think. Now, Alice." He opened a drawer and took out the brooch, wrapped in a silk handkerchief. They studied it.

"It doesn't look old enough," Doran said. "Too bright, too . . . well, flashy, for something made all those centuries ago."

"Ninth century. A thousand years or so ago. Well, enamel does last and processes haven't changed greatly. Some of the Egyptian stuff from as far back as Rameses III . . ."

"I want to stay with you tonight." She buried her head against his shoulder. "Henry, please."

Very gently, Henry disengaged her and transferred her from the edge of the high bed to the reproduction chair.

"I want you to stay, my dear, of course I do. But you do know that you're not quite yourself at the moment."

"You mean I'm drunk, I suppose?"

"No. Only that you have drink taken, to use the Irish expression, and it's affected you. It wouldn't be fair of me or kind to you to take advantage of something you'd regret very much tomorrow."

Doran stared bleakly at the unprepossessing features of Jane Seymour. "This has all happened before. At the Crozier, after that dinner we had there. Remember?"

"No," said Henry. "What you need is a good sound sleep. Come on."

At his door she said, "I'm not really smashed. It was because I was so miserable, it takes me that way."

"I know, I could see that when you came back from your telephone call. Night." He kissed her, very lightly, on the lips. The traditional paternal salute on the forehead would somehow not have been in order.

She walked down the corridor a shade unsteadily, aware of it and already ashamed of herself. Stumbling against a small table she knocked off a cast bronze horse, which fell noisily on to the polished oak floor. It would. With a stifled oath Doran replaced it.

A door opened on the half-landing above. It framed a graceful figure in a robe of hyacinth blue, the rich heavy plait unbound, loose on the shoulders: the Blessed Virgin gazing tenderly down on sinners. The Blue Lady of Caxton Manor. Doran mentally kicked herself for having suspected Morven of entertaining Dermid.

"Sorry," she called up. "Slipped. Hope I didn't disturb you."

The angelic form stood motionless until Doran had disappeared, then glided, like a lovely wraith, towards another door.

The walnut bed enclosed Doran and the Cluny lace spread formed itself into a veil between her sleepy self and the events of the evening.

St. Agnes' moon hath set.

Chapter 6

The frozen time

The new day announced itself to Doran with the small tinkle of early morning tea crockery and the soft crisp rustle of a maid's skirts. They wear brown paper underneath, thought Doran through sleep's mists. It's an old stage trick to produce the effect of layers of petticoats.

She roused herself sufficiently to murmur thanks to yet another stunningly pretty girl, perfectly though unobtrusively made up. The curtains parted with a discreet swish, encouraging Doran to unglue her eyelids and prop herself up against the pillows.

Whiteness had streamed into the room, overtopping all its colours. A white glow, almost a glare, pervaded the ceiling. The swing mirror of the dressing table and the pier glass reflected whiteness, the deep pink of the reproduction Morris wallpaper seemed to be paler.

Doran sat up and stared through the window. As far, that is, as could be seen, for a battery of snowflakes was beating against the glass in steady assault. Beyond it was a white expanse of nothing.

All the features of yesterday's view had vanished—stables, outhouses, one end of the lake, trees. Where these features had been could only be guessed at, or what now lay beyond them.

Last night there had been what countryfolk used to call a white-over, but this was something more. Doran drank her tea, bathed in the tiny immaculate bathroom, glad of its warm shades of rose, and dressed in the only day-clothes she had with her, trousers and a brown sweater. Why had she brought no more? But of course, nobody could have guessed that the world was going to change.

A shrill voice reached her from the dining room.

"Two feet of it in twenty-four hours . . . whole villages cut off . . . the children couldn't go to school, nobody could get to work. I'll never *forget*. After that we moved to Ipswich."

This was Mercia Lang, babbling—the only word—to Bert Prinn. She seemed a changed person this morning, as excited as though she were one of the children who couldn't go to school. Her cheeks were very pink and her eyes bright as a mouse's. After breakfast, perhaps she would rush Bert outside to make snowballs and build a snowman with a borrowed pipe and one of the ancient hats from the rack in the hall.

Bert seemed disinclined to share in her glee. He looked even more preoccupied than he had seemed the night before, waiting for the use of the telephone.

The husband and wife, Mr. and Mrs. Blatt, who had been staying in the Lely Room, were glumly browbeating the young waiter.

"My husband simply has to get away this morning for an appointment in London—haven't you, dear."

"That's right. Absolutely essential."

"I'm sorry, sir, but you'll never get your car out in this." He indicated the view from the dining-room windows: it would have done very nicely as a set for *Scott of the Antarctic* apart from the sledges and the huskies. The parked cars were not visible except as amorphous humped shapes.

"Well, call a taxi, then," Mrs. Blatt snapped.

"I'm sorry, madam. No taxi could get out here, and as a

76

matter of fact the phone lines are down." He got the bad news out in a rapid gabble.

Bert Prinn dropped his fork on his plate with a crash. Mercia said, "Oooh! we're cut off!" The Blatts gaped, aghast, at the now blushing waiter.

"I want to see the manager," said the husband.

"Sorry, sir, it was his day off yesterday and he got caught. He's not been able to get in yet, but I'll tell him when—if he does."

Morven drifted in, a fashion model in a hand-knitted sweater of cream Aran wool and perfectly cut olive-green velvet trousers. Her face, innocent of makeup, was radiant and calm. Dermid followed, like a pursuing ghost. He looked terrible. Doran made room for them at her table which was set for four, as were the three other tables. No twosomes this morning, if he had been hoping for that. In a moment Henry appeared and joined them. He greeted Doran as though the previous night's scene had never happened, and she took her cue from him: let diplomatic oblivion cover all. Dermid glared at him. Morven poured tea and coffee for all four.

"So we shall get no punters," she observed. The word sounded odd on her beautiful lips, and in those heather-honey tones.

"So it seems," Doran agreed. "Likewise no transport home. We're stuck, whether we like it or not."

"Do you really think so?" Dermid seemed slightly cheered at the prospect.

"I'm absolutely sure. Deep and thick and even would be an understatement—the Page wouldn't be able to tread in Good King Wenceslaus's footsteps because he'd be over his ears in snow."

"The longest recorded freeze in Britain," pronounced Morven, "was one of thirty-four days at Moor House, Cumbria, from Christmas 1962."

"Good gracious," Henry said. "How on earth do you know that?"

"I looked it up in the library on the way down. I like to know things, you see." Doran stole a glance at Henry. He had called *her* the biggest show-off he knew.

"I've always been told that Scots education was superior. Obviously their thirst for knowledge is, too," he said, smiling.

"Morven is absolutely brilliant," put in Dermid eagerly. "She got a First in Ancient History and her memory's totally encyclopedic. And she's a quite remarkable sculptress—she had a piece in an exhibition in Glasgow City Art Gallery."

"Dermid, don't," Morven said gently.

"Why not, dearest? I know you wouldn't tell them this yourself, but"—he looked proudly round the company— "she's a skilled fencer, as well, a Maîtresse d'Épée." He stared hard at Henry, as if defying him to prove otherwise. Henry looked embarrassed as he skillfully beheaded his boiled egg.

Doran, too, felt embarrassed. To break the awkward atmosphere she asked, "What's the story behind your name, Morven? It's lovely, and so unusual—in fact I've never met one before."

"I was born in Morven. On the shores of Loch Linnhe, in the shade of Fuar Bheinn."

"Goodness, how romantic." Doran's mind wandered off along Jacobite trails. But it would be tactless to discuss such things with a Campbell. "Yours is pretty unusual too, Dermid."

"Yes. In Gaelic it means lack of envy. Or jealousy. Or desire. I think that's pretty ironic, myself." He shot a meaning glance at Morven, who went on elegantly and imperviously eating bacon, egg and mushrooms.

Oh dear, Doran thought. Why can't the man grow up and stop mooning in public? But perhaps he was genuinely not

78

well, as ill as he looked, not merely sick of love. After all, Keats's illness was the reason behind his terrible jealous letters to Fanny. Consumption took its victims in odd ways, it could make them madly erotic or madly cheerful.

Lydgate came into the dining room, pausing by their table. "I gather we're sequestered by snow." He might have been graciously informing them of something they couldn't otherwise know.

Henry looked amused. "If that's the word. I thought sequestering was what Parliament did to Royalist houses in the Civil War."

"It has a variety of meanings," returned Lydgate stiffly.

"Including, in Scottish law, the seizure of a bankrupt's property," added Morven.

Lydgate ignored her. "Sequestered by snow," he repeated, savouring the phrase. "Walled up alive, so to speak."

Before anyone could comment on the unpleasant vision this conjured up Prinn had come over to their table, leaving his breakfast unfinished.

"Are they still saying that?" he asked Lydgate. "That we can't get away? But it's ridiculous. And the telephone lines—surely there's more than one, in a place like this?"

"Obviously," said Henry, "but they all meet up at the same point, one would imagine. Engineers, as they say, are working to repair the fault. We hope."

Prinn looked ready to burst into tears. "But I must get in touch with—someone. It's absolutely vital. Haven't they got any skis here? I could manage on them—I think—as far as the village. Done a bit of winter sporting in Switzerland."

"Alas," said Morven, "they have equipment for croquet, clay pigeon shooting, hot-air ballooning and gliding, among the more usual pastimes. But not, so far as I know, skiing."

Mercia, listening, giggled. "Bert slaloming down the drive, slap bang, wallop, what a picture! Wish I'd brought a camera."

"It's not funny," Prinn snapped at her.

"Sorry."

Lydgate interrupted smoothly. "I fear you'll have to do as the rest of us, make the best of our sequestration. There are ways of using such interludes profitably: I intend to do that myself. In fact, I shall be glad of the time to carry out a postponed plan of mine." He sounded exactly as he did in his erudite remarks addressed to radio and television microphones, almost a caricature of the public Lydgate.

"Perhaps you could give us some pointers," suggested Henry. The sarcasm was not lost on Lydgate.

"Why should I? All leisure may be creative. Or destructive. Choose which you will." He moved away from them with his peculiar walk, which was stiff-necked and yet had an unpleasing suggestion of a sway in it.

There had been something nasty about the whole exchange.

Somehow she was not inclined to discuss it with Henry. Last night was too near. And, though the thought was not a happy one, he might be part of whatever was nasty in that room, unlikely though it seemed. She hardly knew him. They had known each other for a very short time, years ago, and since then for one day. There had seemed to be something between him and Lydgate—challenge, mockery? When he rose to leave the table she gave him a vague smile. Soon after, Morven also left. Dermid, muttering something, followed.

"Old fossil," said Mercia, glowering at Lydgate's back. "What sort of plan has *he* got? Nothing very nice, I'll bet. I wouldn't trust my kids with him, would you, Bert?"

Prinn looked shifty, and murmured that he wouldn't trust them with anyone much these days. Doran reflected that the housewifely Mercia was a most unlikely authority on weapons of war. Yet she had seen her in action over a good percussion cap pistol, which would have been worth much money if it had kept its mate, and a pathetic battered naval sword with its anchor almost gone and half its hilt missing. She knew all about both items, summed them up concisely, and sent the owners away feeling that they had objects worth keeping if not marketable.

Yes, Mrs. Lang must be more intelligent than she looked and sounded.

Prinn was staring wistfully out at the snow. "Think it's as heavy as it was? Might be just a freak. By lunchtime things could be moving again."

Doran asked a passing waiter if he had heard a weather forecast.

"Yes, madam, a few minutes ago. No sign of it letting up, they say."

"Was there anything about my part of the world—Abbotsbourne?"

"Nearly all that valley's cut off already, madam. They're managing to keep the coast road open, that's all."

"Thank you. You seem to be on your own this morning—are you?"

"That's right. A good few of us live out—they've not been able to get here, so there's only five live-in staff and the breakfast cook." He hastened off. Doran drifted away from the table, through the panelled inner hall, to the marble hall where the Roadshow should now be starting up on its second day.

It was cheerlessly bare. Its own furnishings had not yet been restored, the experts' empty tables were a poor substitute for them. The Labradors were absent, though some zealot had lit the fire. Doran shivered as the front door let in a blast of icy air, and Howell.

He was speckled with snow, flakes lodging in his eyebrows and moustache. Swearing fluently, he slammed the door and kicked off a pair of snow-caked boots some four sizes too big for him.

81

"You may laugh," he snarled, "you go out there and see what it's like. Bloody terrible."

"I know, I didn't mean to laugh, but you look like the Santa who failed the audition. Where did you find those incredible boots?"

"Didn't find 'em. Man lent me 'em, cottage next to stables. Wife ran me up some breakfast, but it wasn't enough. Still serving, are they?"

"I shouldn't think so, but they'll find you something, they're very kind. I shouldn't say you've had one breakfast already. What's it really like out?"

"If they was to empty a million feather-beds up there"— he pointed to the livid sky—"an' every feather had a stone in it, an' you had to wade through the lot, that's what it's like, see."

"Highly poetical. Worthy of whoever won the Eisteddfod. Well, I shan't be going out, and I doubt if anyone else will. See that sort of lump over there? That might be your car: or it might not. We're all in the same boat."

Reality began to dawn on Howell. He was separated from his estate car, only recently acquired second-hand after a roughish career, and at its best no beauty. But it was spacious, he'd had the dog-grid removed to make more room for furniture, it made him independent of Doran's car and of their van. He could sleep off a few beers in it, throw fag-packets and ice-cream wrappers on the floor, make as much mess as he liked, without bringing wails of protest from Andrew—or whoever succeeded Andrew at Reefers Cottage. He had come to look on his car as a second home.

"You mean we're stuck? It's goin' on like this?"

"Well, I've no exclusive information, but to judge by the weather forecast, yes. You and I and the other Experts are marooned here with a few of those charming waiting maids and footmen. The manager and the chef haven't arrived, Miss Pell stayed with a friend for the night, so she isn't here either.

Not to mention that the public certainly won't be able to make it, so no Roadshow.''

''What about my Yank chair? How's Charlie goin' to pick it up, in this?''

''I've no idea—and don't look as if you blamed me for the whole thing.''

Even Howell, ever ready to complain, could find nobody to blame. It was not worth swearing at the elements, which took no notice.

''What we goin' to do?''

''I've no idea what you're going to do. Personally, I'm going to have a good snoop round the house. One doesn't often get the chance to examine a stately home's antiques at close quarters, and at leisure. They've got some very nice things, if you look beyond the portable ones.''

''Everything's portable. I knew a guy had a pair of caryatids in his yard, eight foot high, stone, weighed tons. Got nicked one night, nobody ever knew how.''

''Well, don't let's brood about that. Howell . . .''

''What? I want my breakfast.'' Doran followed him on his hurried progress to the dining room, catching up with him as he sat down firmly at a table and summoned the young waiter, who had just finished clearing. Adding to his points for a martyr's crown, the waiter patiently trotted off for coffee and toast. Doran sat down beside Howell.

''Don't smoke that filthy fag in here,'' she told him, ''it smells like sulphuretted hydrogen, they won't like it. I just wanted to ask you—what do you know about Lydgate?''

Was it imagination, or did a shutter come down behind his eyes?

''Told you yesterday, didn't I?''

''Yes, and you called him a rum bird. He was in here talking to the others at breakfast, and purely on instinct *I* should call him a sinister bird. He said he had some sort of plan, a postponed plan, for using his time here—and something about leisure being both creative and destructive. What do you think he meant?''

"How should I know?'' Howell stuffed his mouth with toast.

"You seemed to be getting on well with him at dinner last night.''

"Yeah. Interesting chap.''

Obviously she was getting nowhere. She changed the conversation.

"I had another look at the Saxon thing last night.''

"Oh yeah?'' He shot her a beady look, at which she blushed, and hurried on.

"What do you think of it? You didn't seem to be taking an interest, but I bet you've got views.''

Howell chewed and swallowed. '' 's a wrong 'un, innit.''

"How do you know? You never even went near it.''

"I know a moody when I see it. Thing like that, just walkin' in with a punter? Either it's as fake as hell or some nutter nicked it from a museum, in which case you leave it alone, see. You don't want to handle hot stuff, *merch*.''

Doran knew well that Howell was not above handling hot stuff if there was enough profit in it for him.

"But the gold's real,'' she said. "It's all real. How would a very ordinary man, which Henry said he was, get hold of . . .''

Howell laid down his knife. "And how do you know there was any man? What if your dear old pal Henry pulled it out of his pocket, where it'd been dozin' all the time, and flashed it around with a fancy tale about some man or other?''

"I thought you liked Henry. At least, I did until last night, and then I thought you didn't like him monopolizing me.''

"I know you,'' Howell said darkly. "Guys can twist you round their little fingers, if you like the way they look and they're old enough to be your dad.''

"Thanks. What it's got to do with you I can't imagine.''

She pushed back her chair. "I'm starting on my tour now—see you around the house. Have a nice day, if you can think of anything to do."

From Howell's disconsolate expression it seemed unlikely that he could.

A strange atmosphere pervaded the Manor. It was as though the silence of the white wastes outside had crept indoors, hushing sounds: what sounds there were. With so many of the staff missing there were few voices. The hum of the vacuum cleaner was still. Passing the television room Doran looked in. Sets of figures flashed on and off the screen, as a loud and very unscholastic voice talked to schools about the economy. Three people were gathered round it—the Blatts and Mercia, watching with absolutely blank expressions.

Curious to be in a house where there were more faces in picture frames than outside them. Portraits which were very good reproductions or copies of classic paintings, portraits with no relevance to this very English scene: Neapolitan flower-girls, Spanish gypsies: portraits, large and once important, of people whom Doran guessed to have no relevance either. Impressive in the clothes they had chosen to be painted in, they looked down, haughtily or distantly. People who had meant something and belonged somewhere, and now were meaningless, their identities left behind in salerooms.

Doran paused before one. It hung on the window-wall of the Long Drawing Room, a life-size painting in a heavy gilt frame.

"Well," she said, "and who might *you* be?"

The young lady was no more than twenty-five. In 1830 or thereabouts she had been dressed for winter sports—ice skating on real ice—all in white; a huge white cartwheel bonnet lined with pleated satin, a pelisse whose champagne-bottle shoulders sloped into enormous ballooned sleeves ending in tight cuffs. The white silk of the pelisse had darkened to cream with time, but here and there glints of white shone out, producing a shimmering effect, like sunshine on ripples. Or like some other material, which escaped Doran.

The skater leaned back, away from the artist, almost as if recoiling from him, clutching an ermine muff against her bosom. The extreme slenderness of her waist and hips was cleverly revealed under those voluminous clothes. Her face wore a most curious expression—coquetry? invitation? fear? It was as if she were writhing away out of the painter's reach (though that was hardly an elegant description of a young lady's action).

"Isn't it like?" said a voice behind Doran. She turned to see Dermid Scance.

"Like? Like whom?"

"Morven, of course."

"Oh." Doran took another look. The oval face, the creamy skin with the bloom of youth and health on it, the dark sleek hair and full dark eyes were certainly similar—perhaps it was a type. The slight, fascinating cast in Morven's left eye was absent, of course, but . . .

"Yes," she agreed. "Quite like, now you mention it. Such an odd way for a sitter to pose. Almost—I really don't know, but it *is* odd. She looks as though she'd make a good ghost, if you know what I mean." She hurried on, anxious to distract him from his obsessive topic. "Do you think there's a ghost here? I should doubt it, with all these comings and goings and lights. They don't like lights, you know— electricity pales the poor things and takes their colour away, hence so many Grey Ladies instead of Blue Ladies or whatever."

Dermid smiled faintly. "I haven't noticed any. Perhaps yesterday's corpse will return in spirit form."

"Mm . . . to the parking area outside the kitchens? Boring for him. Of course, he may have come into the house first. Nobody knows, or anything about him, and now I shan't hear—'' She stopped. She was not going to give away her call to Sam Eastry, even to this harmless young man. "How are you going to pass your time?" she asked, instead.

"I don't know. Mor—other people seem to be in their rooms."

A figure materialized in the doorway near them, and hovered in a melancholy fashion. It was not the ghost of the winter sporting lady, but Howell, palely loitering in a setting which held no prospect of a quick deal. Doran was visited by a bright idea.

"Why don't we—you and I and Howell—go round all the clocks in the house? Just for fun, to pass the time, and let me learn from two real experts?"

"Never called me an expert before," Howell grumbled, but was ready enough to agree. Dermid seemed pleased. He was probably the kind of man who likes being told what to do by a woman.

The Manor held many surfaces, ledges, mantelpieces, shelves, tables. On most of them there was a clock; Doran counted four in one room, not to mention long-cases in the passages. None of the clocks was on the level of the Edward East, the superb brass weight-driven alarm bracket clock which had led Doran and Howell into a mesh of crime the previous summer, but every one had character.

Doran guessed that the two men would have talked them through in every detail, even if they had been the commonest of timepieces, just as two cat-mad persons would have gone through a cat show stopping at every cage. Dermid and Howell shared, it seemed, a contempt for the French Empire type dominated by gilt cupids, nymphs or minor deities. Those were not what clocks were about, not serious clocks. What concerned them were escapements, foliots, anchors, racks and snails, barbrels and cocks. And other even more esoteric terms.

Patiently Doran followed them round from clock to clock.

She knew plenty about clocks superficially, in the way of trade, but this was a crash course. It taught her more about the two men than about clocks. Howell was a clock man, of course, just as someone else might be a porcelain man or an eighteenth-century furniture man. She had never heard him talk at length before, with such erudition and—yes, passion.

Dermid had so far only registered with her as infatuated, depressive and what might be termed wet. Now he appeared as the expert he was, knowledgeable above his years as he discoursed and argued about Black Forest 8-days, American drop-dials, Act of Parliaments and the sort of clocks Doran associated with leaving-presents from firms to clerks, in far-off days. What do they give now, she wondered? The mind boggles.

Dermid was a different person from the young man who had raved gloomily at her in the library. She discovered that she liked him. He had a rather fetching habit of tossing back a lock of hair out of his eyes—which she now saw were an attractive and unusual dark blue, set in thick lashes. She hoped he was not as ill as he looked.

She reproved herself for lingering on male attractions. It was because of the hurt at the back of her mind, because Rodney had not telephoned her, had hardly spoken of her since she left home. If she could believe Helena. Now there was no telephone, and the breach must be getting wider. It was like a tooth abscess, lulled with oil of cloves but threatening agony.

Dermid was talking about a particularly nasty clock of wood and celluloid in the form of a leering Bonzo Dog.

''That will be a treasure in a few years—probably is now.''

''Stuff that,'' said Howell. ''Shouldn't be on a Jacobean dresser, should it.''

''I expect they keep it there as some sort of joke.''

Voices were audible on a landing, the male one rising to

88

a shout. They turned a corner and found Bert Prinn haranguing a flushed young maid.

"I've got to get away, can't you get that into your head? Do something, tell someone!"

"But it's nothing to do with me, sir—"

"Blast it, is everybody in this bloody place stupid?"

The girl cowered back against a stair rail. Howell interposed.

"Calm down, mate, cool it. Not her fault. Want the gel to fall downstairs, do you?"

Prinn looked abashed. "Sorry, I didn't meant to shout. It's just that I can't believe all the telephones are cut off and I need to phone."

The girl rallied. "Don't we all, Mr. Prinn? You're no worse off than any of us."

"Sorry. Sorry. Only you don't understand . . ." He went quickly, shoulders hunched in frustration. The girl gave a spirited toss of her frill-crowned head and vanished down the stairs.

There's a desperate man, Doran thought. Why?

They had moved into the room used as an upstairs leisure place, offering magazines and boxed games, a dart board, a pile of jigsaws, a snooker table. Dermid gasped, a sound wrung out of him. In one of the long window recesses Morven was standing in a lovely, classical, unselfconscious attitude, her hands raised to touch something that hung below the curtain rail. Doran glanced at Dermid, and saw that he had changed back from a horologist to a martyr of love.

Morven turned to smile at them. "You're managing to pass the time, then? How lucky we are to be marooned in a house like this."

"Very," Doran said. "It might have been a railway hotel or a disused Methodist chapel. Have you found anything special?"

"I'm just rather pleased with this." Deftly she unhooked

a ball of silvery glass from the end of the chain that had held it suspended. Doran recognized it as what is popularly called a witch ball, a sphere of glass probably from the Nailsea factory, silvered on the inside. Witch balls had started off as cottage ornaments in the early nineteenth century, not, as popular tradition maintained, as safeguards against the entry of witches through windows.

"Very nice," she said. "So often the silvering's worn off, leaving it all pitted. That one's almost perfect."

Morven was caressing it between those hands which were not almost perfect but quite perfect, to the last dimple and polished nail-shell. "Yes. Quite early, about 1840. I like these better than the coloured, marbled ones." She stroked and turned it, making it reflect quaint distorted convex images of the room and the people in it.

Dermid gulped. "The modern ones . . . not really witch balls, things fishermen use. You can buy them at the sea . . . seaside. I can't remember what they're called."

"Net floats," supplied Doran crisply. It was embarrassingly like seeing a man transformed, turned into a grovelling beast at the feet of Circe. She was angry with him and sorry for him. It was unfair to be angry with Morven, who was only being her natural self. "You could set up in a crystal-gazing booth on a pier, with one of those," she said.

"Telling fortunes. Yes. I could indeed. I am a *taibhsear*."

"A what?"

It was, surprisingly, Howell who understood. "She's got second sight. *Dewines*, she is. That's what she says."

"I was born above the Highland Line, and I have the Sight, sometimes. A gift or a curse, as you look at it. My grandmother had it, but not my mother. If I had a daughter she would probably not have it. I use it very seldom."

She was about to hook the witch ball back into place when Doran asked, "Will you look in the crystal for me, Morven?"

90

Silly, but why not? Why not take the chance of a Sibyl's-eye view on her problems?

Morven looked surprised, but said gravely, "If you wish." She put the glass ball into Doran's hands, left it there for a few moments, then took it back. Doran glanced aside at the men's faces, Dermid's worshipful, Howell's blackly disapproving. She suppressed an urge to crane over and see what Morven saw, with those dark eyes which had gone blank, in the left one the cast more noticeable than usual.

"An empty chair," Morven said at last, flatly. "A fire unlit. Cold." She shivered. "Empty hearth and empty heart . . ."

Doran, too, was shivering. She put out a hand. "Thank you—no more, please."

Dermid half-whispered, "Tell mine."

"No."

"Why not?"

"Don't ask me . . . I will not." The Highland accent was strong over the Edinburgh.

"Loads of balls," murmured Howell as they moved on.

"Witch balls," Doran answered. "Quite different."

* * *

The day was over. The snow continued and came steadily down, the cold intensified. Outside the Manor the vista was one of pure, unearthly beauty, one great whiteness. *All bloodless lay the untrodden snow. He giveth snow like wool.*

Within the Manor the staff calculated how long the food in the freezers might last them and how long the fuel in the log-baskets and the one accessible woodpile might stretch before emergency electric fires were brought out. The pre-dinner drinks were pounced on, evidence of a world still civilized. A Martini, pronounced perfect, was mixed for Mercia, whose elation seemed to have subsided, a double Scotch apiece for Howell and Prinn, tonic with bitters for Dermid, a chilled Chablis for Doran, who could have done with something stronger but preferred to keep absolutely sober. She failed to notice what Lydgate ordered, and was drinking silently, sunk into a wing chair away from the rest of them.

When Henry joined them her heart gave a startled leap, shocking her. She met his smile with her own tremulous one. He joined her beneath the painting of the Skater.

"Got through the day all right?"

"So-so. You?"

"I had a lot to catch up with. Fortunately most of it was in my briefcase. And their library's pretty good. What's the matter with Bert? That's his second double while I've been here. And you're not enjoying that—whatever it is. Let me get you something else. Vodka. I remember you saying you'd never tasted vodka. We were at the—Mitre, Golden Cross? One or the other. I told you to drink it straight down and you did, and choked."

"I remember. And you didn't laugh, though everyone else did."

His hand closed over hers; she let it stay. A sudden, palpable silence fell on the room, leaving only the faint tactful strains of taped baroque music.

"An angel flying over," Henry murmured. Doran turned to him, wanting to say there's something bad here, tell me it's nothing to do with you because I must have you left to believe in . . .

The young barman, who had vanished from his background of gleaming bottles, returned dramatically, lifting the bar flap and erupting among them like a Genie.

"Ladies and gentlemen—great news, the telephone lines have been repaired!"

He was almost felled by the velocity of Bert Prinn's rush past him towards the public instrument in the hall. Mercia was behind him. Politely shrugging, he added, "And there's a call for Miss Doran Fairweather. Would you like to take it in Reception, madam?"

It would look silly to imitate Bert's speed, like a clip from the Keystone Cops. Doran tried to walk sedately to the reception desk, her pulse rate up and excited colour in her cheeks. So he hadn't lost a minute in telephoning her. She would say she was sorry for the other night and everything would be all right again.

Snatching up the telephone she said breathlessly, "Rodney darling. I hoped you'd . . ."

There was the shortest of embarrassed pauses before the voice at the other end said, "It's Sam Eastry, Doran."

"Oh."

"Sorry. But I've found out what you wanted. The chap's death wasn't heart failure, he was—helped. Hard to trace, but they think it was pressure on the carotids, old army trick."

"Ah. Have they found out who he was?"

"Antique dealer. One Reg Haslem of Brighton—shop in Thornhill Street. Trade Only, that's what you people say, isn't it? Can't tell you any more now, hope it's some use to you. By the way, I've . . ."

They were cut off. Doran hung up. She was bitterly disappointed on the one hand, vastly intrigued on the other. Her instinct had been right again: it had been murder.

Chapter 7

Who's the cheater now?

The vicarage number was engaged. Twice during dinner she apologized to Henry and tried again, with the same result. Parish claims on Rodney's time, no doubt, that explained it. (But he could have snatched a moment to make a call himself . . .)

What would have been a markedly silent meal was enlivened by the waiter's thoughtful switching on a tape of Handel's Concerto Grosso in D major.

Henry raised his head from his indifferent food (the breakfast cook was no cordon blue) to listen appreciatively.

"Not pop, not Europop, not shrieking vocals that put you off your food, but actual classical music, carefully chosen for us."

"Elegant, pure and aerial minds," Doran murmured. Henry looked blank.

"Sorry?"

"Keats. Not one of his better days."

"You seem very fond of Keats."

"There's something about the set-up here that keeps reminding me of him and his life story."

"May I ask what?"

"Well. Dermid and Morven. He's quite like Keats to look at. And there's the same passionate, obsessive love on his part.'

"And on hers?"

"No idea. At least she seems to treat him kindly, she's a very gracious person. And even if she reciprocated madly it wouldn't be enough for him, that sort of love never gets enough of what it wants. It would devour the love-object if it could, and still demand more. You did drop a hint about all this when you brought them here—you must know details I don't.''

"Actually no. I've only met him professionally and my acquaintance with Morven doesn't tell me very much about her except that she's a lady who wouldn't settle for second best. Perhaps that's the answer.''

"Perhaps. What about her husband?''

Henry shrugged. "They're divorced, and whatever went wrong happened in Scotland. She's an enigmatic character, very private. I shouldn't try to find out too much about her if I were you, Doran. You've a very inquiring mind, haven't you?''

Doran decided not to tell Henry, nice and charming though he was, what dark places her inquiring mind had led her into in the past. She said, "Naturally, I don't want to pry. But I sort of sense tragedy in the air. Dermid strikes me as a natural-born suicide—if whatever's wrong with him doesn't kill him first. I suppose vicar's wives do get a feeling for that sort of thing, and even in our small parish we've had some sad cases, since I've been the vicaress.''

"How long is that?''

"Last August.''

Henry fell silent, moving the salt-cellar round like a chess-piece. At length he said, "So you're still a bride.''

"I suppose I am.'' A fateful exchange. To Henry a wife—somebody else's—would be one thing, a bride quite another. They exchanged a look of understanding: Doran felt a strange sense of relief.

"Hadn't you better try your home number again?'' he suggested.

"If you don't mind."

The number was still engaged. Goaded, she dialled the operator service, who came back to her with the news that they were unable to get a reply and had reported the number as out of order. "But the engineers won't be able to do anything tonight."

In the Long Drawing Room the small company had scattered itself on various chairs and sofas. Enforced confinement didn't make for sociability. Henry had taken his briefcase into the Writing Room to do some work. Howell had gravitated to the Television Room, where he was slumped with a pint tankard and a new packet of Camels at his elbow, glumly staring at a sequence of camera shots of blocked lanes, silent town centres, stranded travellers huddled in pubs, farmers struggling out to bewildered sheep. Doran, looking in, sniffed. "I've always wondered what the atmosphere in a fox's earth would be like." He gave her the V-sign. Bert Prinn was not to be seen—telephoning again, doubtless—and Dermid was for once not with Morven. She was reading: perhaps he had been graciously asked to give her a break from his attentions. He was playing Trivial Pursuit with Mercia: neither seemed to be concentrating hard on the game. Mercia frequently glanced up at the door, Dermid's gaze wandered towards the sofa which allowed him just a glimpse of the top of Morven's head.

Lydgate sat alone by the fire. He looked like an audience, Doran thought, waiting for the curtain to go up. When would the play begin for him?

She drifted, purposely, towards Morven, perched herself on a low chair beside the middle fireplace (the room had no less than three) and allowed herself to look as dejected as she felt. As she hoped, after a few moments Morven looked up, took in the situation and spoke. Her manners were faultless, her voice, when she spoke, was soft with the kindness Doran had seen in her attitude to Dermid.

"Something's the matter. Can I help?"

Doran blinked away what could easily have been real tears, if she had let them gather.

"Oh. That's a very kind thought. But—it's just that I can't get through to my husband on the telephone. They say it's out of order, but I can't understand . . ." She sniffed.

Morven patted the sofa. "Come and sit by me. Tell me all about it."

Rather surprising herself, Doran did tell this intelligent sympathetic listener more than she had meant to tell, and felt a response when she mentioned the quarrel and the cold parting.

"*To be wroth with one we love Doth work like madness in the brain.* I know."

"From experience? Sorry, that's an impertinent question."

Morven shook her head. "No need. And if it helps to know that you're not alone, I did suffer sorrow and parting." Her words were as poignant as the sound of a pipe lament drifting across the mists of a Highland glen. Doran said nothing. She had never expected confidences from this enigmatic creature, and here they were, unsolicited—or almost unsolicited.

"My husband and I married after a long time of doubt—on his part. I had no doubts. I wanted to be his wife. But he was not sure. And then at last I had the wish of my heart, we were married. I was very happy. Until—he was seduced away from me. By his old—love."

"And—he never came back?"

"No more." *No more, no more, no more, Macrimmon, Macrimmon no more shall return forever.* It was like a knell sounding over the dead on Culloden Moor. Doran was shocked out of her own trouble. This was something worse, deeper and darker. And what kind of woman could have attracted a man away from Morven?

97

She asked, feeling like a million banal television interviewers, "What is there left for you now?"

Morven was staring into the fire, her eyes as blank as when she had gazed into the crystal witch ball. "Anger. Great anger. And loss. But not emptiness. I thank God for my good brain and the work I did at university. I have so much, my knowledge and my skills. Only not the one thing."

Empty hearth and empty heart. That was what she had seen for Doran in the crystal. Doran was suddenly as cold as though the arctic night had pierced the walls and surrounded them. Thinking of Dermid, she said, "You might fall in love again."

Morven gave the bitterest of laughs. "Love is Death." Suddenly she seemed to change from a tragic goddess to a highly civilized, polite human being. "Why am I going over old history to you? You have problems of your own. If I said anything to depress you when I looked in that witch ball, please forget it. Sometimes I see true, sometimes not. I'm sure your husband will contact you very soon."

She picked up her book: the interview—or audience—was over. Doran took the hint and moved on.

Poor Dermid, she thought, what a woman to fall for; not a Fanny Brawne, young, tender, untouched by life. But Keats had called Fanny at first meeting *beautiful and elegant, graceful . . . fashionable and strange*—Morven Cair was certainly that. Doran tried to picture her rival. Probably some fool of a girl without two sensible thoughts to rub together. Too much intelligence could be a fault in a wife.

Had Rodney found that?

To distract herself from that thought she paused by the table where Dermid and Mercia were still playing Trivial Pursuit. Mercia jumped like a shot rabbit; Dermid fixed on her a searching, questing look. Because she had just been talking to Morven, of course.

"How are you making out?" Doran asked. "Gracious

what . . ." she had been going to say "silly questions." She changed it to ". . . a range of subjects."

"You ought to do very well with it," Mercia said, a trifle cattily. "You're always quoting poetry and stuff."

"Ah. But like Sherlock Holmes, my knowledge of politics, geology, chemistry and the solar systems is nil."

They looked blank. Mercia asked, "Is it still snowing? The weatherman said it was going to stop."

"It was snowing last time I looked out."

It had been a beautiful, frightening prospect, a landscape sculptured in snow, as though a new Ice Age were creeping up on the world. The bleak midwinter.

"It reminds me," Doran said, "of those plastic balls children used to get in their stockings at Christmas. There was a snowman figure inside, or a miniature castle or something and when you shook it snowflakes fell. I used to love those, but nobody ever gave me one. You can still get paperweights like that."

"My little girl's got one, only it's a robin inside," said Mercia, and burst into tears.

Dermid jumped up and put an arm around her shoulder. "No, no," he said, "don't, don't." He pulled a watch from his pocket and consulted it wildly, as though knowing the time by a fine John Jones half-hunter would solve the whole problem. Morven rose from her couch on one elbow, a fine statuary attitude, Lydgate merely turned his Roman head to look. Bert Prinn appeared in the doorway.

"What's up?"

"Mercia's a little upset," said Doran. "Understandable."

Morven spoke, a Sibyl pronouncing. "Would it not be a distraction if Henry were to show us his Saxon find again? Debate refreshes the mind."

They agreed, even the sniffling Mercia, that it would be a good idea. Doran went to fetch Henry, still working on documents. He appeared dubious.

"If that's what they want, I'll bring it down, though I don't see much point."

"It can't do any harm, at least. I'll get Howell."

Howell growled at being dragged from the old war film he was now watching. "Told you what I think. And I just got comfortable. Bugger off."

"No, I won't. You wished yourself on this Roadshow—you can just come and join in."

The object which purported to be a royal Saxon jewel lay in the middle of a card table, its brilliant colours set off by the dull green baize. Its viewers stood at gaze: like cows looking over a fence, Doran thought.

"So," said Lydgate, "no word from the member of the public who brought in this—alleged—piece of antiquity?"

"No. I hardly expected there would be," Henry answered shortly.

"He might at least have telephoned, this—very ordinary man, I think you said?—out of curiosity, cupidity?"

"Yes," Mercia put in, "they're always so anxious to know what it's worth, that's what they come for."

Henry frowned. "I don't suppose it's occurred to him. He may not even be on the telephone. I can tell you one thing: I rang the Ashmolean this afternoon and they told me definitely that no reproductions of the Alfred Jewel had been made for sale to the public, and that to the best of their knowledge nothing like it exists. They seemed excited at the idea that there might be something as similar as this."

"Did they add," asked Lydgate smoothly, "that a female likeness of ninth-century date would be highly improbable?"

"Bloody impossible," said Howell.

"No, they didn't. But I take the point." Henry appeared restive. "This speculation seems to me to be getting nowhere. As soon as things return to normal I'll have it assessed properly, that's all I can say."

Doran was visited by an inspiration. "Morven—why don't

you use your gift of the Sight to tell us something about it?''
She explained to the others, ''Morven can sometimes see
into the future—she did it this afternoon, with a witch ball,
didn't she, Dermid?'' He nodded reverently. ''So perhaps
you can see into the past, too, Morven? I mean, the future
of a thing like this wouldn't be too interesting, but its history
would.''

''Ah. That would be psychometry,'' Morven said. ''I can't
claim to do that. But I'll try, if you wish.'' Among sceptical
murmurs she picked up the jewel, leaned back on her couch,
and held the thing in her hands, against her breast. She began
to draw deep breaths. Her eyes were closed. Nobody spoke.
From a distance came the voice of a weather forecaster, his
words inaudible.

At last Morven said, ''It speaks to me. It lay . . . in the
earth. Not far from here. The sea was near. Swampland.
Ships . . . dragon ships. Helmed men. Women. Braids—
ropes of hair. Little children, many little children. Men talking. A tall man, fair. A young man at his side . . .''

She opened her eyes, shook her head dazedly, and replaced the jewel on the card table. ''That's all.''

''Fantastic,'' Mercia breathed. Dermid's face was devout.
Nobody else said anything. Suddenly Morven slumped back,
her eyes shut again, her head turned to one side. She looked
like a weary Madonna. In an instant Dermid was at her side,
holding her, begging her to revive, issuing wild orders for
brandy. She stirred, smiling faintly, and sat up against his
shoulder.

''I'm all right. Just a wee bit drained.''

''Well,'' pronounced Henry, ''that was pretty impressive.
I don't know much about the paranormal, or supernormal or
whatever it's called, but I think it convinced me.''

''Wonder if she can do it with other things?'' Bert Prinn
said. He took a photograph out of his wallet. Doran, craning

her neck, could see that it was of a woman. "Have a go at this, Morven."

Dermid waved him away. "Leave her alone. Can't you see she's exhausted?" He murmured passionate comfort into Morven's hair.

Mercia hovered, then burst out, "I don't care—when she's better I shall ask her to do it for me! I *need* my fortune telling."

Lydgate had risen to his feet. Positioned in the centre of the hearthrug, he surveyed them all with a half-smile, then said, looking at nobody in particular, *"Ad populum phaleras, ego te intus et in cute novi."*

Doran's school Latin still lingered: she recognized some words, but others escaped her. *To the people . . . something, I . . .*

"Please translate," she said to Lydgate. "Some of us are a bit rusty on the classics."

He raised a disdainful eyebrow. "I hardly imagined Persius would be your everyday reading. A noted satirist of the first century AD for your better information. I'll be a little more colloquial: *colubrem in sinu fovemus.* Now, surely, somebody recognizes that really quite common saying?"

Nobody gave any sign of recognizing it. Henry was clearly angry. "You're being abominably patronizing, Lydgate. I'd drop it if I were you. If we need our brains testing we'll know where to come, otherwise kindly keep your classical allusions to yourself."

Mercia giggled. "Yes, why don't you go on *Mastermind*?"

"Furthermore," added Henry, "I believe you're getting at one of us, possibly more than one. If you are, wouldn't it be fairer to come out with it, and give the person a chance to defend themselves?"

Lydgate smiled. "Wouldn't that be rather too simple?

Surely people in our situation should pass the time in playing games; I'm merely giving you all the chance to join in."

"Any game you play's likely to be a dirty one, Lydgate. I have a good memory too, you see."

"Not as good as mine, I think."

It was like watching two tomcats squaring up to each other, Doran felt. She was slightly disappointed when Henry abruptly turned his back and strode out of the room.

The others dispersed. Mercia returned to *Trivial Pursuit*, though her gaze strayed to the reclining figure of Morven. After a moment Prinn sat down beside her. They talked in low voices. Howell was smirking.

"Well, what about that for a load of old codswallop? Didn't I say, didn't I tell you it was all balls, that crystal stuff?"

"Yes, you did, and I haven't any answer, except please don't translate either codswallop or balls into Welsh for me—I'm still narked at not understanding Latin, a language I've been taught. Though Welsh owes a lot to Latin, doesn't it—have you a word like *colubrem*?"

Howell pondered. "*Colomen?* That means pigeon. *Colwyn*—that's a puppy. Any use?"

"Puppy Bay, how fascinating. No, I doubt if either pigeons or puppies have much to do with this situation."

Howell pointed. "Look, old Henry's left his priceless loot behind."

Doran started to say that she would take it to him, then stopped. It might be a mistake to find herself in the Holbein Room again. Morven, removing her hand gently from Dermid's, said languidly, "You take it to him, Dermid. Now I can still feel its vibrations."

Reluctantly he left her side. Doran watched him pick up the jewel and hold it in both hands as Morven had done: caressing his lady by proxy, no doubt. For a long time he held it and looked at it, his face intent. Perhaps it was speaking to him, as well. Sadly, even tragically, she guessed. And significantly.

"Want a game of poker?" Howell was asking.

"No, thanks. I've got to look something up in the library."

"Okay." He wandered off towards the kitchens. Some of the depleted staff might not be averse to a little harmless play. Howell fancied himself as a Mississippi gambling dude of the *Showboat* era: Gaylord Evans.

When Doran finally left the library she carried a little-used volume. Since Keats's poems seemed to crop up so much at present, it might be as well to refresh one's memory. She had been lucky enough to "do" him for school A levels, and to become slightly infatuated with him as a person. In his brilliant, short life he had managed to turn out a lot of work which might repay study in the present case.

It did: and so did a row of encyclopedias and dictionaries.

From the few uncurtained windows on stairs and landing leading to her room the prospect was majestically dazzling, a snow scene which might have been created by some giant stage designer for a *Nutcracker* Spectacular, the Kingdom of Sweets all done in icing sugar.

Through the window where the staircase turned towards the house-front sounds from outside indicated activity. Across the drive, and in the lane which led twistingly to the village, men were working with shovels. Somehow a JCB digger had been coaxed to the scene, where it was rhythmically digging up and flinging out snow like a domesticated Triceratops, the huge prehistoric reptile with the three-horned frilly head.

Doran watched, fascinated. How had so many humans and this mechanical giant been got together and put to work in such conditions? Pointless to ask. The fact remained that the powers behind the Manor had combined to free the house from the spell of the snow. Where solid whiteness had been a faint path appeared. If the men and the Triceratops worked all night it might well extend to the front door by morning.

One of the young maids was leaving Doran's room. She looked tired.

"Oh, madam, I've been making the fire up in your room, but I'm afraid there's not much wood left—they can't get any more in till they've cleared a path to it."

"That's all right, I'm going straight to bed anyway. How are you managing, with so few of you here?"

"Well, we've just about got round, but that's all. Hopefully some of them'll get through in the morning. At least we're off duty now."

"Good, about time. Where do you sleep?"

"In the attics—they're really nice, beautifully modernized, only tonight it's bitterly cold up there, with the central heating down."

"I'd noticed. Well, put an extra blanket on and have a good sleep."

"Thank you, madam, I will—and you."

In bed, Doran, like Keats's Madeline, trembled in her soft and chilly nest. Her two hot-water bottles were tepid; she missed Rodney's comforting presence. All evening she had tried not to think about the unanswered telephone and his failure to make a call to her. Why? Why? Was there really a fault, or had he taken the phone off the hook?

I will *not* think about it any more, she resolved. Not until morning. Joy cometh in the morning: we hope.

A relief to switch on to the discoveries she had made in the last two hours. Thank God for a mystery. She lined up her facts, and the queries they raised.

1. Morven had only claimed occasional flashes of second sight, yet on request had been able to demonstrate instant psychometry, the deduction of an object's background from contact with it.

2. The "vision" Morven had said she had seen, of the jewel lying in swampland, in a place not far away—near dragon ships, men wearing helms, women with braided hair, and children—tied up neatly with what Doran had discovered in the library. In AD 893 a Danish fleet had crossed to England from the Continent. Most of the Danes had settled at Appledore, not an hour's car journey southwards from the Manor. Appledore verged on the Romney Marshes.

3. The Danish warriors, wearing horned helms, had sailed in dragon-headed Viking ships, with their wives and children: they intended to settle in the district. Their women were usually portrayed wearing their hair in long plaits.

4. A tall, fair man, and a young man at his side? Well, King Alfred was fair, according to the colouring of the original Alfred Jewel. And he had a son, Edward, who attacked and defeated the Appledore Danes. So far so good, on the psychic front.

But all this information was readily available in the library at the Manor. Morven could have looked it up in preparation for doing just this act.

If it was an act; and somebody thought it was. With difficulty Doran had found the quotation from the learned Persius. It meant *Show your medals off to the public as much as you like—I know you, inside and outside.* So Lydgate had no illusions about Morven's psychic powers.

And his quotation? It meant *We are cherishing a serpent in our bosom.*

Was Morven the serpent? What about *Keat*'s female serpent? (Now *there* was a find.) Or was there another one? Henry and Lydgate seemed to have had a feud at some time. Why had Henry said, in front of them all, that he believed in Morven's "vision?"

What was the meaning of Dermid's expression, as he held the jewel? Was he puzzled? Troubled?

And why were Mercia and Bert behaving so oddly? Why . . .

Doran realized, with finality, that she was not going to be able to sleep without a hot drink. At home they would have had a nightcap of Scotch with almost boiling water and a teaspoonful of honey. She could hardly hope for that, but the Scotch might be possible. Somewhere below stairs Howell might still be awake, perhaps still playing poker. He could always be relied on to have a bottle or flask on his person. They could find a kettle and boil it.

Even to one wearing a thermal dressing gown and slippers, the landing was cold. Of course, the maid had said the central heating was down, and even the lights which were left on all night seemed dim, ghostly.

A flight of four stairs, leading upwards, brought her up short. She had never seen them before, that was for sure. On the wall at her right a realistic and gruesome painting of dead game was also new to her. The glazed eyes of pheasant and hare leered at her as she passed.

She had obviously taken a wrong turn, coming out of her door. But it was hardly worth going back, there was certain to be a way down to the main hall from this direction.

At the top of the four steps a further corridor stretched ahead. At the end of it a flash of long frilled pinafore told her that another overworked maid was still about. She called out softly, "Can I get down to the . . ." But the girl had vanished.

There were room names on porcelain plaques, the doors close to each other, indicating small single rooms, called after male notabilities, Prince Rupert, Samuel Palmer, William Byrd, Beau Nash. These must be the Bachelors' Rooms, in Edwardian times stark little apartments used by the single gentlemen guests at house parties. Bert Prinn had called his room mean, because it had no telephone.

Beyond Beau Nash the corridor petered out. Doran turned a corner and met a blast of icy air, so piercing that she hugged the dressing gown round herself, in vain. *Bitter chill*, indeed. "Oh, do hush, John Keats!" she said aloud, more for reassurance than anything else. Though, oddly enough, it would have been less alarming to find that slim shade walking beside her than to be there alone, in the unnatural chill and dim light. He had been a natural-born defender of the weak, a rescuer of tormented kittens and younger boys. And women. *Why should women suffer?* he had asked.

He wouldn't have thought her cowardly to be feeling so unreasonably nervous. Nervous about what? She had taken a wrong turn at her bedroom door—all that was needed was to go back and start again.

The landing ended in a long window, almost a french door. It was open, the lower half of it pushed up as far as it would go, the curtains blown inwards to drape themselves limply over the low sill. What lunatic had opened it? Teeth chattering, she ran to pull down the sash.

Snow had come in, a white spatter on the red runner carpet. Outside the window she saw, with a violent shock, something long and dark beyond the sill, a man's body lying face downwards on a flat roof. Scarlet stains made a red spatter on the white carpet of snow.

Doran screamed, a scream ear-piercing enough to wake the dead. But the man in the snow lay still.

Chapter 8

A sharp knife to the bone

Later it would strike her as a very feeble, conventional way of reacting, and she would be ashamed of herself. But at the time such thoughts did not stop her screaming uninhibitedly all the way to the top of the main staircase.

There were lights and voices, running footsteps, people appearing like rabbits popping up from burrows. Someone had an arm round her—Henry: everyone was asking what was the matter. She tried to tell them, but her breath had run out. A pallid, alarmed face materialized before her—Dermid.

"Oh, good," she said. "I thought it was you."

"Thought what was me?"

"The body. On the roof."

She was in a chair, drinking water eagerly because her mouth was dry (so that was why people in books always called for water in emergencies).

"Take it easy," Henry was saying. Morven was rubbing her icy hands in a most professional way. Three young girls and two young men were asking each other who had the key of the bar grill. All looked most un-Victorian in assorted nightwear. The receptionist, Yvonne, a haughty young blonde who had kept to herself throughout the past two days, turned out to have hair long enough to sit on. The breakfast cook, Mrs. Rapton, a harassed little creature of middle age, had forgotten to put her teeth in and was hovering as inconspicuously as possible.

Doran drained the glass of water and put it down.

"It's all right—I mean I'm all right, I had a shock, that's all, and I think someone ought to go and investigate." She told them as clearly as she could what she had found, and where, to the accompaniment of gasps, cries, and squeals from the girls.

"I'll go," said one of the footmen. "Come on, Terry, better be two of us."

"I think we'd all be warmer in the hall," said the sensible Morven. "The fire should be still in there. Can you walk, Doran?"

Doran said she could, but held on to Henry's arm because she was still trembling with a combination of cold and shock. The trembling began to subside when she was settled by the fire, which Henry was feeding with sticks and small logs. The three girls, who proved to be called Sara, Tiggy and Perdita (wouldn't you know) scuttled about organizing coffee and wine.

"We could mull it," suggested Tiggy. "All you need is lemon and cinnamon and nutmeg, and I know where there's some brandy for emergencies."

All agreed this was a good idea. While the beverages were brewing Doran relaxed and took in the appearance of her companions. Henry, rumpled, like a disturbed owl, with an unbecoming growth of white stubble on his chin. Oh dear. Dermid, absolutely ghastly, as though he hadn't slept at all. He might have stood in for that leading character in the Scottish play, who had just murdered Sleep—nobody else, one hoped. Morven, in a sleek dressing gown of black velvet with a gold edging, hair falling long and dark on her shoulders, the contours of her face childishly soft.

And nobody else. No Mercia, no Prinn, no Lydgate, no Howell. Then who . . . ?

It was an inexpressible relief to see Howell's head, then the rest of him, appear jerkily from the basement staircase behind the reception desk, like the Demon King rising to stage level on a faulty trap. He wove an uncertain way towards them.

"You look terrible," Doran greeted him. "What have you been doing? No, don't answer that."

"That guy, lent me the boots, he came over, see, wanted to know if I'd be sleepin' in the stables. Then another guy came in from the dig-out and we had a drink."

"So I see."

"What's up, then, what you all sittin' down here for?"

"The young lady's found a body," volunteered the breakfast cook semi-articulately.

"We don't know that it's a body." Henry sounded irritable. "You may have been quite wrong, Doran. It was probably one of the diggers from the drive, securing a window, who was overcome by the cold on the roof."

"Then why hadn't he been overcome by the cold in the drive?"

Before anyone could produce a theory the footmen returned. Both appeared shaken. John, the tall one, usually calm and self-confident, spoke hesitantly.

"He . . . he *was* dead. There was . . . a knife wound. In the left shoulder. Quite a lot of blood."

The boy Terry turned a greenish colour and left hurriedly.

Out of the shocked silence Henry asked, "Who was it?"

"One of your party, sir. One of the experts. Mr. Lydgate."

Morven crossed herself. Interesting, thought Doran. Dermid turned even paler than usual, if that was possible. The breakfast cook squealed. Tiggy dropped the cup she was holding with a crash that shattered it on the marble floor. The other girls, their composure temporarily disturbed, moved nearer together, even the haughty Yvonne. Henry looked shocked but not, perhaps, surprised. Howell said, *"Duw."*

Doran took a deep breath: somebody had to be in charge, and it was not her first experience of murder.

"I hope you didn't move him, John," she said, "or touch anything the police might want to see."

"Oh no, madame, I do know better than to do that, from all the—well, the crime programmes. We did just lift him to see who it was, then we put him back as he had been when we found him." He gulped. "We left the window untouched because of fingerprints."

"Good. Now, I think—if you agree, the rest of you—that we ought to ask John to go and fetch the others, Mercia and Bert—er, Mrs. Lang and Mr. Prinn."

There was a murmur of agreement. "Must have cloth ears, both of 'em, sleepin' through this lot," said Howell. Doran organized the girls into making more coffee and mulling more wine, then said to Yvonne, "We'll have to telephone the police at once. Would you like to do it, as you're staff, or shall I?"

"Please . . . if you would. It's a bit different from—what I usually do." She smiled nervously, not her normal Sloaney self. Murder had a way of transforming personalities, lifting off the mask of whatever one chose to show the world. Since John and Terry had brought the news they were all different.

Doran went to the telephone switchboard on the reception desk. "Of course, it will take time, getting the police here . . ."

John reappeared, breathless. "They're not there. The beds haven't been slept in, neither Charlotte Brönte's nor Prince Rupert's."

Doran was too startled to ponder on the curious vision this combination suggested.

"But they must be somewhere about. Perhaps they're . . . we'll have to go and search. I'll go, for one." The girls made brave, helpless noises. "We know where to look. We don't mind." But it was obvious that, underneath their impeccable façade of sophistication, they were frightened. Young Terry had returned, very pale now instead of green. Doran commandeered him and Yvonne, as being likely to know the building better than guests.

It was, she thought wildly, like the search for the missing Mistletoe Bough bride. They might well seek for Mercia and Bert till a year passed away, without finding any sign of them. She was not looking forward to possible gruesome discoveries. They were not in the most likely places, the Leisure Room, where, on that mad night, one would hardly have been surprised to find them playing snooker. They were not in any of the empty rooms used by the live-out maids and footmen, on the top floor, or in the library, the so-called Smoking Room, or any of the bedrooms at present disused, for which master keys had to be found.

They were certainly not in the Lely Room, but the marooned Blatts were, in bed, having slept through it all, volubly indignant at being aroused. The search party left with threats of solicitors' letters ringing in their ears.

The missing couple were not in the area of the kitchens, laundry, the integral garage used by the hotel owners when at home, the staff washrooms or the Dog Room. The two Labradors arose from their comfortable baskets beside an all-night stove. They were not in the least indignant at being aroused, but delighted. Their long dull night had been broken up by beloved humans, who would now caress and entertain them until morning.

Doran gently disillusioned them. "No, sorry. Pity you're not bloodhounds."

"They're awful, Briar and Rose," Yvonne said. "Great soft things. They'll make a fuss of anybody. Daddy's are just the same, totally adolescent."

"Don't you think," Terry suggested timidly, "we ought

113

to look again in Mrs. Lang's and Mr. Prinn's rooms, madam? They might have left something behind that would be a—clue,'' he ended proudly.

"Brilliant thought, Terry. Why didn't it occur to me?" Because, she knew, for all her woman-at-the-helm pose she was shocked and discomposed and—yes, frightened. Altogether at her lowest ebb, one way and another. Never mind that, there was investigation to be done.

In the bedrooms of the absent pair a close look revealed that neither coats nor outdoor shoes or boots were in the wardrobes, nor anything in the way of luggage. It was impossible to tell which of their other possessions were gone, but there was an impression in both rooms of hasty flight. Terry emerged from Bert's bathroom.

"No razor," he said. "No shaving stuff at all. And his pyjamas were laid out on the bed. I know, because I did it, as the maids weren't here."

"So Mrs. Lang's nightdress would have been put out, too. We'll check that with the girls. And no bags of any kind."

"They've skipped," Terry said. "Cleared off. Somehow."

Yvonne frowned. "*And* not paid for their extras."

Doran was back in another, poetic night flight—on St. Agnes's Eve. *"And they are gone; ay, ages long ago These lovers fled away into the storm,"* she murmured.

"Pardon?" said Terry.

"Lovers?" said Yvonne. "You mean they were? I didn't notice, and I generally do. And they had separate rooms . . ."

"Oh, I don't know, I've no idea. Sorry, I was just thinking aloud. Well, at least that solves one question."

Both understood her. At least they were not looking for two more corpses. They returned to the group by the fire in the hall. Nobody seemed to have moved, though coffee cups and wine glasses had obviously been refilled. The girls were yawning, the breakfast cook unbeautifully asleep, poor thing, with her toothless mouth open. Doran woke her and dismissed all the staff to their beds, except Yvonne.

"The men digging outside," she said. "How did they get there, and who were they?"

"Oh, just the lads from the village. That earth-shifter's kept at the farm and they've got a couple of four-wheel drives. I rang them as soon as the lines came back. God knows how they got through that snow, but they managed it two winters ago when we had a thick fall. The Boss has got it organized. Can I go now?"

So they were left, the five experts. Morven seemed withdrawn, brooding, the cast in her eye quite pronounced, her crystal-gazer's look. Dermid was sitting as close to her as possible, his eyes hardly leaving her face.

Henry was smoking, something Doran had never known him do before. He must have found some of the cigarettes kept for guests rash enough to use them. He looked deeply unhappy.

"I suppose," Doran said, "they haven't taken anything valuable? Have you checked on the—the Saxon thing, Henry?"

"I locked it in my case this evening. They'd hardly have skipped with that."

Howell seemed to have found his second wind, and a supply of cans of McEwan's ale. His noxious cigarette smoke mingled horribly with Henry's.

"I'm going to phone the police now," Doran said. "At least we know the score about Mercia and Bert. Not lost, but gone before. Oh, never mind."

A voice from the Eastgate night desk answered briskly, took down particulars of the death and disappearances, asked intelligent questions, assured Doran that inquiries would be put in hand immediately and that someone would be with them as soon as possible.

"That won't be very soon, surely, in these conditions."

"As soon as possible," repeated the brisk voice. "Please be sure not to move anything before they arrive." Click.

Doran repeated the desk clerk's words. "He sounded confident enough. But I don't see how anyone can get here, unless they take the wings of the morning."

"Whatever that may mean," muttered Henry.

"Well, come on," Doran said. "Instead of sitting there like birds of ill omen, why don't you tell me anything I don't know about the late Falk Lydgate? He was just a face on the box to me till I got here, but I gather you both knew him before he, er, dropped off the perch. Well? Morven?"

Morven slowly shook her head. "He was a malcontent. They do no good to man or beast . . . or themselves."

"Malcontent." Doran dredged in her capacious memory and came up with a fairly obscure play of that title by a dramatist whose works had deservedly not graced the English stage for at least two hundred years. For once she had no quote or comment to hand. "Ah," she said. "Yes. He did give me that impression. Dermid?"

"I hated him. Better dead, in my opinion. I wish I'd killed him, but I didn't."

Doran let this sink into her consciousness. Then, "Howell?" she said.

Howell crossed his ankles and threw away a smouldering stub.

"Yeah, I'd met him—I told you. Few times, not to say knew the guy well. In my league, in a manner of speakin'."

Doran was fully aware that this did not refer to taste, expertise or anything connected with antique dealing. "Ah, that. He was—"

"Gay. Thought it stood out a mile—didn't it?"

"Actually, no. Now you tell me, I see it." She recalled her thought about the swaying hips. "But—not a particular friend?"

"You know Andrew?" Indeed she did, that frail blond-

116

to-colourless creature. Andrew would, she imagined, have been rather frightened of Lydgate. How extraordinary, they were talking as if they were alone, in front of all-but strangers.

"Lydgate wasn't our type," Howell was saying. "Rough trade. Know what I mean?"

Doran did. So, to judge by their expressions, did Dermid and Morven. Both looked shocked and sickened. A little moan came from Morven. She turned her head and buried her face in Dermid's shoulder. His arms went round her and held her tightly to him.

Henry rose abruptly to his feet, angry. "What in God's name's going on? I've no idea what Lydgate's private morals have to do with the fact that he was murdered in this house tonight, but I for one don't intend to sit here listening to them being discussed. I'm sick to death of the whole thing, and tired out. I'm going to bed."

"Henry," said Doran, "you haven't told us your own feelings about Lydgate."

He turned at the door. "*De mortuis* aside, I think he was in a . . . But you're as brilliant in Anglo-Saxon as you are in everything else, aren't you, Doran? Supply the word yourself. Good night."

In the wide grate the remaining logs were glowing only fitfully, turning to white ash. A sudden spatter of drops from the chimney sent up a flame. The snow was creeping into the Manor.

"I think we'd all better go to bed," Doran said. "I'll switch on my room extension in case anyone rings."

"Thank you," said Dermid. "You're being wonderful." He smiled, a sudden bewitching smile that illuminated his face: and, for Doran, his personality. He gently raised Morven and led her out, saying a quiet good night for them both.

"I hope so much it isn't him," Doran said.

"Fancy him as well, do you?" inquired Howell wearily.

"No, I don't. I don't fancy anyone except my husband. I've just been feeling very insecure. Never mind about me. I was only saying that I like Dermid Scance, and I'm sorry for him. I think he's a victim, in a way."

"What of?"

She shrugged. "You name it. Love? Illness? The late Lydgate?"

"Think they were both in it, then, those two—knockin' off Lydgate?"

"No, I don't, in the slightest. And anyway, we all seem to have forgotten about the first murder, the man in the car park."

"Murder? News to me. Heart attack, wasn't it?"

Doran told him what Sam had said on the telephone. "So, you see, we've got two murders and two mysterious disappearances."

Howell mused. "Reg Haslem of Brighton . . . no, don't think I know him. Blast this bloody snow! If it weren't for that I could get down there and find out. Eastgate, even—Arthur Hidley would know, he's in with all those types. I remember a guy used to have a shop down Spring Gardens . . ."

"Yes, I'm sure. Howell—don't you think it was curious, how those two reacted when you mentioned Lydgate and rough trade? Morven looked absolutely shattered, and Dermid nearly as bad. Why? I mean, it isn't nice, the idea of picking up . . ." She felt herself turning pink. "Well, sailors in ports and, er, male prostitutes and things in pubs and, er, elsewhere, but it's not actually criminal, is it . . . and not anything that would affect them."

Howell was regarding her with a fond, pitying smile.

"Don't you worry your head about it, *merch*. Takes different people different ways. You push off to bed and get some sleep."

"I think I will. Where will you be? You could have one of the Bachelors' Rooms."

Howell shuddered. "No thanks." They both pictured what still lay at the end of that corridor: frozen now, on this bitter night, and a drift piled above it. "I'll kip down in that place off the kitchen, ought to be a butler's pantry only they don't have a butler since the last one quit. Sleep tight, now."

"I doubt it." She gave him a light kiss. When she looked back from the top of the staircase he was putting a heavy iron guard round what remained of the fire.

She awoke from what had seemed a dream-ridden, fever-ish sleep. But it had lasted six hours, and the light that bounced off the white glare outside belonged to early morning.

After a shower and a cup of tea from the equipment thoughtfully provided in her room, the events of the night before seemed entirely unreal. Looking out, she saw that the workers of the previous night had done an astonishingly good job of clearing the drive with the aid of their faithful Tricer-atops. It was still there, its tall head lowered, as if waiting for someone to bring it a nosebag.

Beyond it, a visible path extended down the long drive leading towards the village. It was obvious that Mercia and Bert would have been able to get away that far, at least, with a struggle.

There seemed a change in the landscape. But of course— it was no longer snowing. The first purity of untouched whiteness was gone, the battleship-grey skies sending down no more flakes. As Doran breathed on a windowpane, then rubbed it clear, a lump of congealed snow fell past it to the sill.

Outside her room there was no sign of life; only faint stirrings came from other parts of the house. She went down-stairs. The dining room was empty, the tables unlaid, but from the kitchens beyond wafted the fragrance of frying ba-con.

Tiggy and Perdita were there, scuttling about, leaden-eyed but immaculately costumed and made up.

"Mrs. Rapton's not very well this morning," Perdita explained, "so we said she must stay in bed and we'd do the breakfasts. Sara's looking after her."

"You're trained cooks as well, then?"

Both smiled, the faint superior seraphic smiles of girls who were doubtless also trained to groom a horse, run up a high-fashion model for royalty, operate a word processor without using a single oath and set about rebuilding a house should it chance to fall down. In no time at all they had a full English breakfast on the table for Doran. The Blatts appeared, still bad-tempered from the midnight invasion of their bedroom, and inclined to blame the two girls for the whole thing, snow and all.

Henry joined Doran. He was calm and formal this morning, only seriously concerned with the necessity of wearing the same shirt two days running.

Tiggy missed nothing. "That's all right, sir—if you'll leave it outside your room after breakfast I'll have it washed and ironed for you in half an hour, if you can manage till then."

Henry said that he could, and that he was more than grateful. To Doran he said, "Aren't they marvellous? We're pretty lucky, in some ways."

"Some ways. Though I feel like the man in that sad poem of—What's-his-name's—I never shall love the snow again. Shan't even like it, in fact." But of course Henry didn't like being quoted at: she switched the conversation to the relative virtues of thick and thin marmalade.

Neither Morven nor Dermid appeared. Doran wondered if they were together, until she heard Perdita telling Tiggy that Mr. Scance had rung down to Reception for some breakfast in his room, and that Sara was to knock at Mrs. Cair's door when she'd settled down Mrs. Rapton. "No newspaper of course for Mrs. R., poor dear, and she does hate not to have her *Sun*. Take her a women's mag from the hall.''

So Dermid was not still consoling his love. Doran was unsure whether she was glad or sorry.

"Henry," she began, "that Saxon thing, and what Morven said she saw. I think I ought to tell you . . .''

Perdita, by a window, gave a sharp loud cry.

"A plane—coming this way! No, it isn't—Tiggy, look, it's . . .''

The sky above the Manor grounds was filled with the unmistakable buzz and rattle of a helicopter. They rushed to the window, crowding each other, to see the giant insect-form fly over the house, circle and descend on the acre of concrete which was its landing pad beyond the north garden. Men scrambled out of it, muffled-up forms who walked through the snow at surprising speed.

"Seven-league boots, obviously," said Henry. "If this is police efficiency I salute it. How on earth did they—''

There were voices, men talking as they came through the back door of the kitchens, and into the dining room. Those at the window hurried to meet them.

And Doran, with a shriek of joy, fell into Rodney's arms.

Chapter 9

Human Serpentry

"There, there, there. Now, now, now." Rodney was patting her shoulders rhythmically and forcefully. "Don't take on so, pray. I just came for the ride—and to see how you were."

Doran detached herself reluctantly. "I'm all right—now. Gracious, what a sight you look. Whatever have you got on?"

"Everything." It seemed so, indeed. An enormous padded coat which looked as though it had seen both world wars topped a padded jacket, shiny waterproof trousers, and glimpses of at least three sweaters. A grey knitted scarf which looked none too clean was wound round his head, hood-like. The one item missing from his wardrobe was a dog collar.

Rodney glanced down approvingly at his swaddled form. "I hoped I looked like Biggles."

"More the First Man on the Moon, from where I'm standing." She was unwinding the scarf to reveal a tousled head. "Where on earth did you get all this clobber?"

"Eastgate nick. Sam and I went down there last night to find out what the state of play was round here." Sam Eastry, one of the police personnel now milling about the room, heard his name and sent Doran a cheerful salute.

Rodney had no intention of disclosing just how he came to be at the Manor: he preferred not to think about it himself. He had not known about the restoration of the telephone lines the previous evening. His attempts to telephone Doran at the Manor had been baffled by the continued "unobtainable" signal which they had been receiving all day. It was not until mid evening and a local television news bulletin that he heard the truth, and noted Helena's nervous air. She had been trying to divert him to another channel, so as to miss the news.

Without a word to her he went to her bedroom. A telephone extension had been put in beside the bed, in case she had one of her bouts of illness. It was off the hook.

When he confronted her Helena made no attempt to deny what she had done. "It was just a joke," she said lamely.

"Oh? I'm not amused."

"I'm sorry, Daddy. Don't hit me."

"If you were a normal healthy girl I would not only hit you, I'd beat you until you couldn't sit down. As it is, I shall have your phone extension taken out as soon as anyone can come to do it. I suppose you realize—but no, of course you don't, having no imagination—that a dying person might have needed me tonight? But then you wouldn't consider a fatal accident or a terminal illness half as important as your pathetic jealousy, would you?

"I seem to think you've been in church when we've recited the Litany. Well, have you?"

"Yes."

"In that case you may recall that in it we ask the Lord to deliver us from envy, hatred and malice and all uncharitableness. It also mentions sedition, privy conspiracy, and hardness of heart, now I come to think of it. Obviously some prayers don't work. I hope you're proud of yourself. Good night."

She watched him go, aghast.

He'd find out that she had taken her telephone off the hook the previous evening, too.

His telephone call to Sam was brief, and his tone less amiable than usual.

"Why the hell didn't you tell me there'd been a murder at the Manor? I do have a faint interest in what happens in the area where my wife happens to be, you know."

"I couldn't, Rodney. The lines only came back a couple of hours ago and when I tried to ring you I couldn't get through—"

"I know, I know. All right. Listen, can you get me to Eastgate? I want to be on the spot if any more news comes through, and if possible I want to get to the Manor myself. Yes, I *can* leave the house—Carole's here on duty."

A four-wheel-drive vehicle, borrowed from a farmer and operated by Sam, appeared miraculously within the hour, outside Bell House. In it they made a maddeningly slow journey down the partially cleared coast road. Sam needed to be at HQ since there was little he could do in Abbotsbourne with only his Honda for transport. He disliked leaving Lydia and Ben beleaguered by snow, but the police house was warm, there was plenty of food in stock, and Ben was a resourceful lad. Lydia had promised not to venture out.

They reached Eastgate well after midnight, all but frozen to their seats. The town streets were negotiable, though only just, the police station a haven of unbelievable warmth and light. Their old acquaintance Detective-Inspector Burnelle was on duty, holding court attended by fat young Detective-Constable Ride, WPC Jo Allison, and a raw constable whom Sam had not met, almost speechless with shyness.

"You're mad, sir, of course," Burnelle cheerfully informed Rodney. "Constable Eastry's journey was in the normal way of duty, but I really think you could have saved yourself the trouble and discomfort. This death at the Manor seems to have no connection with your good lady apart from her having stumbled on the body."

"Literally, I gather. Not pleasant."

"Not altogether, no, but she's a pretty resilient character, so far as I remember. Didn't you telephone the Manor yourself? Surely that would have saved you all this bother."

"No bother," said Rodney tightly.

"Well, well, now you *are* here, have some more tea. I'm afraid it's going to be a rather uneventful night for you—not a lot of incidents expected in the town with conditions like this."

His silent acolyte had barely poured a third cup for all of them when the desk telephone rang.

Ride, swelling even larger with importance, informed them, "There's been another violent death at the Manor, and two unexplained disappearances."

"So," said Rodney to Doran, and Howell who had joined them in the dining room of the Manor, "that's how we come to be here, Burnelle and supporting cast, including, for all I know, Bill Brewer, Jan Stewer, Peter Gurney, Peter Davey, and Uncle Tom Cobbley and all—probably tucked away in the fuselage, if helicopters have fuselages."

"I thought helicopters only carried two or three people at the most."

"Ah, that's common, civilian ones. This is an F76—I think—kindly loaned by the Met. There seems to be very little snow in London, so they got it down here with the greatest of ease, complete with half the Force already in it. I really had no business to ask for a lift, but I somehow talked them round. I said I'd volunteer as police padre if need arose."

"Magic," Doran said. "A magic carpet."

"I've always imagined magic carpets to be comparatively comfortable—whooshing through the warm Persian air so quickly that one didn't notice anything beyond the odd Roc or Singing Tree or here and there a Djinn materializing from a magician's lamp. However, not so, it was so perishing cold that I don't suppose I shall ever be warm again."

His face was, indeed, of a pale purplish colour very unlike its usual healthy tinge, and the hand Doran held was icy.

"Whisky," she suggested, agitated. "Come upstairs and have a hot bath and go straight to bed."

"Willingly. But then so the other travellers should, and it wouldn't be fair. Yes, what can I do for you?" He was addressing a man who was hovering, a tall thin man with a gimlet eye and a slight twist at the end of his aquiline nose.

Doran recognized the hoverer. "Detective-Inspector Ogle," she said. "We met two years ago, didn't we?" Two years ago: he had browbeaten her and all the other witnesses in Abbotsbourne's celebrated murder case, and come to a number of wrong conclusions.

"Chief Inspector," he corrected her mildly. "Based at the Yard now, Miss . . . Mrs. Chelmarsh. They sent me down on this case because of my knowledge of the district."

"Oh. Yes." Perhaps one should say "Good," but it would be hard to infuse the word with much enthusiasm.

"Well, you do seem to have a knack of getting yourself mixed up with some queerish cases, don't you, madam. A couple of murders, a couple of people slipping off into the snow without any means of transport . . . you antique types, you do seem, er, prone to *find* 'em. I expect you knew the deceased well, both deceased?"

Doran was starting to deny this hotly when Burnelle joined them, Ride at his heels, announcing that the police were now going to take statements. Doran looked for the familiar notebook and pen, but to her surprise Ride was opening a tape-recorder. This was the new experimental sophisticated method, Burnelle explained: more sophisticated, but here, on location as it were, they would have to make do with portables.

Another sergeant, Ogle's acolyte, was starting on his lineup of suspects. Henry, in anticipation, seated himself in a rather fine rosewood carver. Doran noticed that his fingers were

126

tapping nervously on its arms, and that he might just as well have been occupying a dentist's chair.

"That's Henry Gore, isn't it?" Rodney asked. "I'm sure I recognize the face."

"Yes." Doran did not elaborate.

Henry would have to wait for his inquisition. The police, from gallantry or some other motive, were questioning the females first.

Hotel premises are singularly well adapted to separate interrogation. Doran saw Morven, the three girls and Mrs. Blatt being led off in different directions, while Ogle requested her to accompany him and Ride to the library.

She looked back at Rodney. "Can't I have my husband with me?"

"Sorry, madam, not policy for non-witnesses to attend an interrogation," Ogle replied with satisfaction. She shook her head at Rodney, who shrugged.

In her previous experience of Ogle she had formed the impression that Ogle was vain, ambitious, unscrupulous, too clever for his own good. So sharp he'll cut himself one day, was the popular expression. Also that he was not above fancying women, but regarded them as hen-witted and poor witnesses. In his presence she had an impulse to exaggerate her speech to cut-glass brittleness and visualize herself as supernaturally tall and frosty-faced.

She hoped this image was getting over to him, but from the first question felt irritation rising, giving her away as all too human.

"So you deny previous knowledge of deceased, Falk Lydgate."

"I deny it because I didn't know him. I'd only seen him on television."

"Isn't that rather strange, as you were in the same profession?"

127

"Not in the least. He was at the top of it and I'm—well, only a few rungs up the ladder."

Ride looked up questioningly. "She means she's near the bottom of the market," Ogle told him irritably.

Doran flared. "I didn't say that. I merely meant that he was an acknowledged expert and I'm just a dealer."

"Ttttt. No offence meant, madam. Well now, so, not knowing deceased, what was your impression of his relationships with the rest of the party?" He consulted a list. "Mr. Gore, Mrs. Cair, Mr. Scance, Mrs. Lang, Mr. Prinn? Did he as it were mix well?"

"I don't think he was a mixer." She was not going to volunteer information about the conversation in the hall after her discovery of Lydgate's body, Dermid's acknowledged hatred, Morven's strange description of him as a malcontent, Howell's frank revelation of his sexual nature. Or Henry's brief brush with him: "Any game you play's likely to be a dirty one . . . I have a good memory too." Let them tell the police themselves what they had felt towards Lydgate.

But, to be helpful, she said, choosing her words with care, "I did think he might have a down on one of us, from something that had happened in the past. There was a sort of covert malice in his manner of speaking, as though the person concerned would understand him, but nobody else."

"Could you make that a bit clearer, madam? Give us an example, for instance, something the deceased actually said?"

"Oh, I don't know. He quoted some Latin and obviously expected someone to understand it."

"Did you?" The question was a whip crack.

Doran looked him straight in the gimlet eyes. "No."

"You surprise me. I thought you were a rather learned sort of a lady." A taunt.

"I suppose I am in some ways," drawled the supernaturally tall frosty-faced person Doran was trying to be. "Not all, however."

"I see." He gestured to Ride, who stopped the tape, paused, and played back Doran's last few words. She was daunted by the unreal sound of her own voice, which was Ogle's intention. He smirked at her clear discomfiture before signalling the resumption of the recording. "Now, your discovery of the bodies."

Doran answered question after searching question. She was aware of being made to feel that she was a glaring example of a bad female witness, that her memory was poor and her powers of observation feeble. She wished very much that she had not been the one to find Lydgate. When, at last, Ogle dismissed her she had become too drained to keep up her pose of loftiness.

"By the way," he said as she was leaving, "we'd be obliged if you didn't discuss Mr. Haslem's death with any of the others, unless you already have. I know what you ladies are for chattering."

"Well, I did happen to mention it at the time." Temper gave her a surge of combative strength. "In spite of the natural garrulity of the female nature I've managed to restrain myself from discussing it since." She swept out before Ogle could reply.

In the corridor she met Morven, under escort. "Torquemada?" Morven asked.

"On the top of his form—pincers, thumbscrews, rack, red-hot irons and the Scavenger's Daughter, all working well. Enjoy yourself."

"Thanks."

Doran wished she could be a fly on the wall to watch Ogle coping with that serene, detached beauty.

She found Rodney drinking instant soup in the dining room, a steaming kettle in the hearth.

"Have some," he said. "Add boiling water only. You look as if you need it."

"Too true. I feel as if I'd been a blood donor above and

beyond the call of duty. Dracula could learn a lot in there. I know it's his job, but of all the odious, snide, repulsive creatures . . . !"

"You don't like him."

"Did you, on that helicopter trip?"

"It was only from Eastgate to here, and I couldn't hear a word anyone said, besides which I was too cold to care. But I take your word for it, anxious though one is to support and encourage the police. Now Burnelle is a decent chap. He talked to me like a father at the Eastgate nick last night, or whenever it was—told me that being mixed up in murder cases didn't necessarily make someone a murderee."

Doran smiled fondly.

"Did you think it did?"

"Well, yes, from previous experience. I just couldn't stand being cooped up at home . . ." His voice died off.

"Why couldn't you get through to me, after the phones came back? And why didn't you answer when I rang the evening before?" Doran asked gently, already having a suspicion of the reason. She could see Rodney making up his mind what to tell her. "Never mind. I expect there was bound to be interference."

"That's what it was—interference. Thank you. Let's forget it. Was it very unpleasant, finding the body?"

"Fairly. Short but sharp. I'd been wandering along the corridors, not really anticipating anything awful but at the back of my mind on the look-out for a ghost in snuff-coloured smalls. And then I felt this cold blast from the open window, and there he was."

"*A traveller, by the faithful hound . . .*"

"Exactly the line that occurred to me."

"*Silent but beautiful he lay?* Or not?"

"Not at all. I didn't care for his looks when he was alive. Still less after . . . What I care for even less is the thought that somebody here killed him. You see, I rather like them all."

"Henry Gore?"

Doran's hand went up to her cheek and dropped again: what a give-away gesture. And after all there was nothing to give away. "I used to know Henry in Oxford, when I was at the shop. We went out once or twice. He's a pleasant person, very civilized. He was nice to me, I enjoyed finding someone here I knew already."

What a blasted perceptive creature you are, she said silently.

Rodney bent his head in agreement, as much with her thought as with what she had said. He felt violent jealous dislike of Henry Gore. But he knew his romantic, susceptible wife well enough to forgive a straying fancy of hers, even before there was anything to forgive. If a man attracted her she would fall for him, though probably not all the way. A man was in no position to criticize, after all. He could see a very faint reflection of himself in Henry: if in the future he met a woman in whom he could see a reflection of Doran, he might well fall for her. Briefly.

The room was empty, but for themselves. Doran glanced round it. "Just before we're invaded, please can I say that it's wonderful, marvellous, unbelievable to have you here. I was so miserable, you know."

"Yes, so was I. I'm sorry I blew up like that."

"I'm sorry I did. All over now."

"All over." Both knew it was not quite true. But to say it was a comfort, and the right thing to do.

"I suppose Bill Gregg thought I was a prize bitch, sweeping out like that?"

Rodney's lips twitched. "He didn't actually mention it." He took off his spectacles and rubbed his face wearily. The lids of his eyes were drooping at the corners more than usual, and there were dark shadows round them, among lines of tiredness. For once he looked more than his years. Doran exclaimed.

"What a selfish wretch I am! You must be exhausted, after last night. What . . . how did you come to be in the helicopter, anyway?"

"Sam gave me a lift to Eastgate. I didn't get a lot of sleep." In fact he had had none at all.

Doran said, "You're going to bed now, this minute. I should have insisted on it before. I'm a fool, and callous with it. Come on."

Rodney surveyed the wide walnut bed approvingly. Normally a tidy dresser and undresser, he dropped his clothes on the floor at random, yawning uncontrollably. Doran prepared a hot-water bottle and tucked him up with it under the Cluny lace bedspread. She watched him fondly until his breathing told her that he was already asleep.

The morning was long and tedious. It seemed impossible that so few police personnel could seem to fill such a large house. The photographer was everywhere, using up apparently inexhaustible stocks of film and highly portable flash equipment. Doubtless the poor fellow moved rapidly to warm himself up, after his first icy assignment outside that open landing window.

Doran had been passing a door of the inner hall when they brought down something long, covered with a blanket, on an improvised stretcher, a ladder they had found. She wondered if they would put him in the Flower Room, where the other corpse had been.

The various subjects of police interrogation returned, one by one. Nobody said very much, as though the questioning had drained them. Doran stationed herself by the heart of the inner hall. Fires were rationed, with fuel in short supply, and this one was a useful central point, near the foot of the staircase and giving on to all the principal ground-floor rooms. From time to time young Terry appeared to inspect it and add more logs. Doran asked him, needlessly, whether the staff was coping.

"Yes, thank you, madam."

"I wouldn't mind a bit giving a hand, if I'd be any use. In the kitchen, perhaps?" She had heard Mrs. Rapton—everybody must have heard Mrs. Rapton—objecting violently to being questioned; and, having been kept by the police for as short an interview as possible, loudly proclaiming at least eighteen times in exactly the same words that she would never, no, never, allow Those Chaps to take down anything she said on That Machine.

"It's very kind of you, madam, but the girls seem quite happy."

They seemed in their element, indeed, the three superb, smooth Sloanes, fresh as daisies in crisp morning uniforms. Coffee was brought to Doran by the fire, with the information that a light buffet lunch would be served from one o'clock.

"Thank you, Tiggy. I hope Mrs. Rapton's well enough to help."

"She's quite all right now, madam. John mixed her a Betsy Ross and it seemed to revive her."

"What's a Betsy Ross? Sounds like a folk song."

"Acksherly, she's supposed to have made the first American flag, in Philadelphia, when the Revolution broke out."

Trust you to know. "And there's a drink named after her?"

"Cocktail, acksherly. It's supposed to be one part brandy one part port with a dash of bitters and half a teaspoon of Cointreau. But John thought Calvados would be better, Mrs. Ross would have drunk applejack, wouldn't she, and Calvados is the nearest. It was ap-solutely funtustic—we all had some." A reminiscent smile crossed Tiggy's perfect features.

"Lovely," said Doran.

After Tiggy's departure nobody seemed anxious to dally with her at her vantage point by the fire. Howell had gone out after breakfast, wearing the borrowed thigh-boots and armed with a pickaxe and a fire shovel. He was determined to disinter his car, which contained supplies of the kind of cigarette he would be unable to get in the hotel, and a bottle of his preferred whisky.

And Doran didn't need him any more, now she had Rodney.

Doran tried to start a conversation with Yvonne, but the receptionist had gone back to her usual place at her desk, where she was engaged with the bookings ledger, disinclined for chatter. The Blatts had retired to the drawing room to sulk. But one wouldn't want to talk to them anyway.

Henry went by with a mechanical smile, briefcase in hand, on his way upstairs. Morven drifted past towards the library, which led off the hall, went in and shut the door after her.

Dermid was not far behind. He hesitated, glanced nervously at Doran, then followed. Doran, without obviously looking up from the magazine on her lap, saw him pause inside the library, as though he had not been welcomed in.

Consumed by irresistible curiosity, she moved to the table on which magazines were laid out, replaced the one she had been reading, picked up another and leafed through it, listening.

"I, er. I wondered if they by any chance had Ree's *Clocks, Watches and Chronometers* on the shelves." This was Dermid, tentative, hopeful. "It's a very old work, of course, but they might just . . ."

"Why not look?" Morven's voice was cool.

"Thanks. I will. I hope I'm not disturbing you."

No answer. Doran moved round the table so that her back was towards the library. She was now nearer to the door. Thanks to her excellent hearing, every word of the softly conducted conversation was now audible.

"Darling, I must speak to you. I didn't want to last night,

134

after you'd been disturbed by that . . . well, by that object of Henry's.''

"No?" Ice, or just detachment?

"And then the Lydgate business in the night. I really didn't want to upset you any more."

"What are you trying to say to me, Dermid?"

A gulp. "The object. The Saxon jewel. I put my lens on it before I gave it back to Henry. Darling, it couldn't be Saxon. I do know something about the technique. I don't go much for fancy watches, but I've got two French ones in my collection, a Dutêtre and a Breguet, and I know them by heart. This thing's transfer-printed, probably on a copper base covered with powdered flint glass and arsenic, which could make it any age. But it's not hand-painted—it couldn't be much earlier than Battersea, say 1750. Brilliantly done, but wrong."

A light musical laugh from Morven. "Powdered glass and arsenic. We seem to be still in the shadow of murder."

His voice was agitated. "I said nothing about murder. Morven, you must have known this—you deal in porcelain, you couldn't have mistaken a modern fake. Because it *is* modern, the Battersea and Bilston factories wouldn't have turned out anything like this. I mean, the *champlevé* process would be . . ."

"Should you not be talking to Henry about this, not to me? It was not I who brought the jewel to everyone's attention."

"I know, I know, I'm sorry. I just wanted to tell you—and to ask you why you went through all that . . . that . . ."

"Performance? Pantomime? Rigmarole?" Then, very gently, "Dermid, you're making yourself ill. Sit down. There, that's better. Have you told anyone else about this?"

"Of course not. Would I tell anyone anything that concerned *you*?"

"Good." Morven had obviously moved nearer. Doran

135

jumped guiltily and retreated round the table. The library door shut off further conversation.

Doran, pretending interest in an ancient number of *Horse and Hound*, heard a polite cough. Sam Eastry was standing by the fire, watching her.

"Oh, Sam." She saw in that kind doggy face the knowledge that she had been at it again, meddling, prying. She felt a betraying blush spreading up from her throat.

"Doran," he said, "don't get mixed up in anything, will you?"

"I don't know what you mean, Sam."

"Oh yes, you do. Two men are dead because of something that's happened in this house. I'd rather you didn't go the same way, just because of liking to find things out, as I can see you're doing at the moment."

"I am not!"

He pointed to *Horse and Hound*. "Thought you were anti-hunting. Changed your mind, have you, staying in a country house? Now come off it, Doran. You've got your husband here and as soon as the road's clear you'll be going back home, and all these people won't matter to you any more."

Doran glanced through a window. The clear panes that framed armorial stained glass were clogged with frozen snow. No more was falling. "So when do we leave?"

Sam frowned. "I don't know any more than you. I wish to God I did."

"What's the matter?" It was not like Sam to complain about conditions on a job, particularly one that took him out of his routine area.

"Nothing's the matter. I want to get out of this place, like everyone else. And don't try to dodge the issue. I'm warning you, don't interfere. You know what's come of it before."

She was about to argue when Ogle strolled in.

"Finished all current business, Sergeant?" He ignored Doran's presence.

"Constable," corrected Sam shortly. Ogle pulled a face of exaggerated astonishment.

"But surely—you've taken promotion since I last had the pleasure of collaborating with you? Why, it must be—two years?"

"No, I haven't . . . sir. It suits me to stay where I am, as community constable."

"Dear me. I wonder what this place Abbotsbourne's got? Should have thought it a bit slow, for an active officer not over the hill yet. Must have some attractions not visible to the naked eye." His tone suggested that Abbotsbourne was well known to be full of callgirls beckoning from pink-lit windows.

Doran chipped in, bristling with annoyance. "Constable Eastry's invaluable to the village. There wouldn't be any bell-ringing at our church if he hadn't organized the ringers, he's President of our Gardeners' Society and he runs a Road Safety campaign in the schools, and . . ." Her voice died away. Not because of any reproachful look from Sam, whose expression was perfectly immobile, or any uttered sneer from Ogle. She knew that she was saying just the things one shouldn't say in front of that man, overweeningly ambitious for himself and contemptuous of humility in others.

The only thing she hadn't said was that Sam's daughter Jane lay in St. Crispin's churchyard; by staying in Abbotsbourne her parents felt still close to her, illogical though that might be.

"Ah. Makes himself generally useful, does he?" commented Ogle, the sneer not even veiled. Doran walked out, not trusting herself to answer.

The buffet lunch was not festive. Clearly the hotel's supplies of fresh food were rapidly running out. Sandwiches were few, because of the shortage of bread, the number of ways in which frozen prawns and smoked salmon can be used are limited. The soups and chili con carne, most in demand, vanished quickly.

The Blatts complained steadily of everything.

Doran made a sortie at the subject which was on her mind.

"Aelhswith. The lady of the jewel. What are you going to do about her, if the man who brought her in doesn't get in touch again?" she asked Henry.

"Not much I can do, is there? But Morven's promised to take it up to town and get a man she knows to look at it. Apparently he's made a detailed study of the period and Saxon jewellery in particular. He ought to welcome a new piece, there's so little of it about, thanks to the eighteenth century's nasty habit of digging up grave-barrows and scattering the contents."

"And if he says it's genuine?"

"I'll have to advertise for the owner. Obviously it can't be sold until he turns up."

"And if it is sold—who profits?"

Henry was clearly irritated by her questions. "You seem very interested in something that isn't your field, my dear." Or your business, his tone implied. "Since you ask, I don't want to profit from it myself, it's up to Morven to take what cut she wants."

Doran struggled with her conscience. On the one hand she badly wanted to warn Henry of Dermid's discovery. But she had only overheard it, and overheard information isn't evidence, like what the girl said to the soldier. She was saved from herself by the voice of Rodney.

"*Good morrow to the day so fair, Good morrow, sir, to you.* And you, my love. Good afternoon would be more accurate, but I feel so refreshed that I address you matutinally, if that's the word I want. *O magic Sleep! O comfortable bird!*"

He was indeed looking very different from the haggard apparition of breakfast time. Bathed, shaven, bright-eyed, wearing a respectable enough blue sweater and a good if crumpled pair of cords, he was a pleasant and cheering sight. And most unlike any clergyman Henry had ever encountered, to judge from his expression.

"You must be Doran's husband." Henry held out his hand.

"Fortunately for me. And you must be Henry Gore. *Aut Gorus aut nullus*. Sorry. My wife tells me you're old friends."

"Fortunately for *me*." The echo was deliberate. They had already sized each other up, and Doran sensed that Rodney, however liberal his principles, instinctively resented Henry and that Henry thought Rodney affected, arrogant, and offensively given to putting people down by esoteric quotations.

"You must be starving," she said to Rodney. "There's not a lot left but I'll get a plate and you can collect. Wine, beer or coffee over there"—she indicated a long table at which John and Sara were bar-tending—"and drinks are on the house." She led him away before the atmosphere could grow frostier.

Since it was not a set lunch they took their plates into the Long Drawing Room, where they could eat in comfort and seclusion. Doran led the way to the end nearest the conservatory, a pretty addition in wrought iron and Victorian stained glass. There they settled on a sofa with a handy small table beside it. The ferny fragrance of the winter hothouse hung on the air like a captured breath of summer.

Other lunchers had thought on the same lines. Morven and Dermid were at the opposite end of the room, out of earshot, talking earnestly, and the Blatts had returned with food to the place where they had been sullenly ensconced for most of the morning.

"Morven Cair and Dermid Scance," Doran said. "Scots and Irish respectively. She's *née* Campbell."

"Very striking. Voluptuous yet spiritual. Sacred and Profane Love. Her friend appears to be on the delicate side. *Youth grows pale, and spectre-thin, and dies . . .* What makes me think of that?''

"Your natural intuition, I expect. La belle dame sans merci certainly has *him* in thrall." She poured out her impressions of them, Dermid's painfully obvious passion, Morven's learning and scholarship, the episode of the witch ball: even the vision Morven had seen in it for her. "*An empty chair. A fire unlit. Empty hearth and empty heart.* What a horrid thing to tell me. Do you suppose it could be true?" She shivered.

Rodney put an arm round her. "Perfectly. But don't worry, dear one, don't think of it again. It's an exact description of me yesterday afternoon. You did say it was afternoon, didn't you? I was practically round the twist at not being able to get in touch with you, too distraught to light the fire, and . . . well, generally not at my best and brightest. That's all it meant."

"Oh. I'm glad." She drew closer into the comforting warmth of his hold. "Then there was the next time she did her second-sight thing. It was yesterday evening." She launched into the story of the arrival of the alleged Saxon jewel and Morven's psychometric "reading" of it. Then, a little hesitantly, confessed her own excursion into spy country, that morning.

"I did listen, frankly. I mean, I can't pretend I couldn't help overhearing, because I deliberately moved to where I could hear better, and I won't say I'm sorry I did—it was most enlightening. I ought to have seen it for myself—it just shows one isn't as expert as one thinks. I absolutely believe Dermid that the jewel's a wrong 'un."

"I've heard you call such pieces naughty, haven't I?"

"That's right. Very naughty, in this case, because someone's gone to the trouble of faking it in a setting of real gold and making it almost irresistible to a collector or a museum. It's amazing how even museum experts can be taken in."

"A good mind behind that, one would say."

"Extremely good, and curious—almost twisted. Which reminds me—come and look." She jumped up, pulling him by the hand.

"Just a minute, I haven't finished my quiche."

"It'll keep. It looks as though it *has* kept, quite a time. I want you to see something."

They were standing in front of the portrait of the young lady Doran had thought of as Winter Sports or Fun on the Ice, 1830. She looked ideally equipped for weathering the drive, beyond the window next to her wrought gilt frame, a landscape of high-piled blue-shadowed snow against a leaden sky.

Rodney stood back, studying the painting, moving about to see it from all angles. He flicked off the nearest lamp-switch, then flicked it on again. He removed his spectacles, polished them, put them back.

"Well?" Doran said.

"The least important question—who is she?"

"Nobody that matters. At least, I supposed it mattered to her. Lady Emily Something, a connection of the family in William IV's time."

"No relation, then, to the lady at the far end of this room, who now has her back to us. No. In fact, there's no real likeness, it's just a look, a type."

"That's what I thought. Tell me what you see in her. Fear? Invitation? Come on, I'm relying on your instinct for character."

"I see evasion," Rodney said. "Duplicity. She's evading the painter's eye in case he sees the outlines of her figure, under all that silk. Evading . . . someone who might see her for what she is."

"Exactly! I knew you'd get it. Do you see anything about her dress—the material?"

"Mm. It glitters, like—a fish's scales?"

"Not a fish," said Doran softly. *"She was a gordian shape of dazzling hue . . . And full of silver moons, that, as she breath'd, Dissolv'd, or brighter shone, or interwreathed Their lustres . . ."*

"Lamia the serpent."

"Lamia. I've been conscious of Keats ever since I came here. Perhaps this is why. You've quoted him yourself twice today, what with comfortable birds and pale youths. I took the *Poems* up to bed with me last night, and I found it then—the clue to what Lydgate had said earlier, in Latin, something that meant *I know you, however you may disguise yourself*, and *We are nourishing a serpent in our bosom*. I read all through the *Poems* apart from the very long ones and when I got to *Lamia* I understood."

Rodney was extremely well acquainted with the works of Keats. He needed no reminder of the classical tale of Lamia, an enchanted snake in love with Lycius, a youth of Corinth. Restored by a god to her woman's shape, she sought out Lycius and married him. But at their wedding feast the old philosopher Apollonius discerned her real nature and denounced her; on which she vanished in an instant.

"I've always felt sorry for Lamia," he said. "After all, she was doing no actual harm, poor thing."

"And it must have been nice being a woman again, after being a serpent, even a beautiful one. And having gone through all that pain to change back—*scarlet pain*, he calls it. I bet he got the details of that from attending childbirths when he was a medical student. I should think he . . ."

Without finishing the sentence Doran turned away from the portrait. Rodney followed her to the sofa where they had been sitting, but left his quiche unfinished.

"You have to be careful with Keats," he said, "too much of him, and one gets haunted. I've had some."

"So have I. I was quite mad about him when I was sixteen or so. Fanny Brawne did say he had some spell that attached people to him, and it seems to have gone on working. Never mind him for the moment. So you think I'm right, and we have a Lamia situation here—Morven is Lamia, Dermid Lycius, and . . ."

". . . and the deceased Lydgate was Apollonius. But who was Haslem, why was he killed in the car park, and how does he come into it?"

"I don't know," Doran said, "yet."

Chapter 10

These lovers fled away

"Tell me about Lydgate," Rodney said. "That may be a problem question, as when the late Queen Mary roused a lady-in-waiting in the middle of the night and demanded, 'I vish you to tell me about Stalin.' Sorry, I can't do the accent, but I believe it was formidably Teutonic."

"I'll have to make do with imagining it. As to Lydgate—well, I hardly knew him, he obviously thought me too small-time to bother with. He wasn't exactly anybody's mate, didn't join in much at drinks time, didn't circulate. He seemed to me to be watching somebody, as though he were waiting for the moment to surprise them—shock them, perhaps. Oh—the only person he seemed to take to at all was Howell."

"Ah."

"Yes, exactly, ah."

"And did he—surprise or shock anyone?"

"Not that I noticed, just rubbed people's fur up the wrong way. Curiously enough, the shock came after he was dead, when Howell opened up about Lydgate's, er, propensities." She described the scene of the revelation. It was a shock to hear about that upper-crust fastidious-looking person consorting with rent-boys and such. Morven and Dermid seemed quite horrified—revolted, I mean. Morven looked as though she was going to be sick."

"A strong puritan streak in both?"

"Shouldn't think so. Morven's a Catholic, and the two

144

don't usually go together. She's also too much of a woman of the world. I don't know much about Dermid."

"I know nothing, of course. But he seems deeply in love—perhaps madly in love, enough to be instantly affected by anything that affects his lady. In fact I'd classify him as an old-fashioned romantic, all for love and that sort of thing. Like, if I may mention the name, Keats. Only Keats was tough in other ways, highly physical, with a reputation for fighting all and sundry when he was a lad and a turn of wit that could be distinctly bawdy. He must have seen plenty round the hospitals in downtown Southwark, and I don't suppose it bothered him too much."

Doran mused. "Dermid looks terribly ill. Do you suppose it could be the same thing, making him as vulnerable as Keats was at the end of his life?"

"Pulmonary tuberculosis? Practically wiped out by the discovery of streptomycin. He wouldn't be allowed to go around in such a state nowadays, spreading infection. No, it's not that. Let's not worry about those two. This bombshell of Howell's: did it explode before the other pair did their escaping act?"

"No, they'd gone by then."

"How did they view Lydgate?"

She shrugged. "Hard to tell. They didn't speak one's language, as it were. I got the impression that Bert Prinn was pretty thick. Mercia Lang seemed on the dim side, as well, but she was bright enough in her own line."

"What was?"

"Arms and armour. Not a bit what you'd expect from a dolly little thing like that."

"Ah. Could she have been bright enough to wield a piece of hardware, as well as knowing about its history?"

"How should I know? But she was distinctly jittery after the punters—the public—arrived for the Roadshow. When the phones came back into operation she was all of a twitter.''

"Waiting for a call?"

Doran considered. "Afraid of getting one, I'd say. I wondered—only wondered—if she'd been told something awful by the first man who was killed, Haslem: I even allowed myself to wonder if she killed him. Whatever was on her mind, Bert knew about it—they were always conspiring in corners. When he wasn't on the telephone himself.''

"To whom?"

"Someone in Northampton, I think."

"Notable as the crime centre of Britain, Northampton? No, merely for boots and shoes and Dr. Doddridge who wrote *O God of Bethel, by whose hand*. Well, *they are gone, ay, ages long ago*, and only the police can discover where. It seems to me, my darling, that we have two most mysterious couples in this case. And Henry."

"Yes, Henry." Doran avoided his eyes. "Henry loathed Lydgate. It was obviously mutual, they'd had a fairly severe quarrel at one time, that was clear.''

"Could the quarrel have had any connection with—rough trade?''

"No!" The denial was so loud and emphatic that Morven and Dermid turned around to look.

"Keep your voice down," Rodney said softly. "All right, I get the point, Henry's totally straight. Do you think he understood Lydgate's Latin dig about serpents in bosoms?''

"He didn't admit to understanding it, but he did get very stroppy and take it as some sort of challenge.''

Rodney was holding an ashtray in the shape of a lily leaf with a frog sitting on it, turning it this way and that as though it were a unique, possibly priceless, work of art.

"So Henry could have been the serpent in question, and all our pretty fancies about the Lady Emily portrait pure raving, induced by an overdose of Keats?''

146

This time Doran met his gaze. "Yes, of course. I'm afraid being shut up here with these people has made me a bit inclined to fancies—pretty or otherwise. That, and worrying about home."

"As to that . . ." Rodney began. He was interrupted by the voice of Ogle's sergeant, from the door nearest to them.

"Would you mind staying where you are, sir, please?" This was to Dermid, who had risen from his chair at Morven's side. "Chief Inspector Ogle wants to see everybody in here for a few minutes."

"Oho," said Doran. "The Inquisition will now sit on the heretics."

"Not much of a day for the bonfire and the stake."

"Just as well. Dermid and Morven are coming over here. Let's be terribly nice to them while keeping our deductive powers firing on all cylinders."

"I'm afraid your metaphors need some attention. See me in the vestry after Evensong."

"Just concentrate on your flair for detecting the diabolical, will you?"

Dermid wore an unaccustomed look of peace and serenity, as though in some happy dream. Morven was looking exceptionally beautiful. She still had on the Aran sweater of cream wool, which had presumably been cleaned overnight by Tiggy's miraculous instant laundry, but the velvet trousers had been exchanged for an elegant kilt of what Doran recognized as the tartan of Campbell of Argyll, a dark green ground with wide black and blue crossings lightened by an overcheck of yellow and white, the pleats held together by an ornamental silver *skean-dhu*, the hilt finely wrought. Seventeenth century? Certainly an improvement on the usual oversized nappy-pin that fastened kilts. Against the dark cloth her lovely hands were perfect as the hands of a marble statue.

Doran saw the frank admiration on Rodney's face and felt a twinge of jealousy. It wasn't fair that anyone should have so much—the looks, the voice, the alluring accent, the brains. And the clothes. How many had the woman brought? How many dressing gowns, especially?

She was chatting to Rodney, to whom she had only been introduced a few moments, with as much ease as though she had known him for years, about religious symbolism in pottery and porcelain. Rodney, who knew next to nothing about it, listened, obviously charmed.

"For some reason religious subjects never fetch as much as secular. With a few exceptions, of course."

"Of course."

Doran couldn't help interrupting snappily, "Any Madonna, with or without Child, is bound to sell. That lovely Enoch Wood—"

"If it *is* Enoch Wood. It was much copied."

Before Doran could launch into an argument the others began to appear: the three girls, John and Terry, the Blatts, puffed up with indignation. Doran heard Mrs. Blatt declaring that she would speak to someone with a bit of influence when they got back to town. Disgraceful treatment, really disgraceful.

Henry came in. Doran hoped he would sit elsewhere than next to her, as he did. Yvonne appeared, clutching a ledger as if determined to show that she was not to be distracted from her work by police frivolities.

Burnelle was behind her. His expression was not frivolous. He strongly resented the man Ogle taking over what should have been his personal investigation, and would have been, but for the blasted snow. Neither Sam, Ride nor any of the other police were present.

Ogle marched in and began by rearranging everybody except Burnelle. The others he directed into a semi-circle with himself as its focus, seated squarely in front of the three girls.

"I bet he's hoping for a good view of their legs," Doran murmured to Rodney.

148

"In those skirts? He won't get even the flicker of a tempestuous petticoat."

As though fully aware of Ogle's intentions, Tiggy, Sara and Perdita sat with their feet demurely together, white aprons prettily in line. Admiring their symmetry, Doran thought of something which immediately eluded her, as Ogle said sharply, "Everyone here? No. Somebody missing. Mr. Evans?"

Doran remembered that she had not seen Howell for some hours. Oh horror. Where had he been, and what doing? The car, of course.

"I'll go and get him," she volunteered, and before anybody could stop her had hurried to the front door.

He was there, in the now well-trodden drive, leaning negligently on what was now recognizably his vehicle, smoking. At her repeated cries and beckonings he came forward, plodding heavily in the great boots. His eyes were swimmy, he was singing. The words of his song, to the tune of "My Bonnie Lies over the Ocean," pierced the clear frosty air.

> My mam *she works hard in a* cath-ty,
> *My* tad *makes* efelychiad *gin,*
> *My* brawd *he sells* cyffyr *at Caerdydd,*
> *My God, how the money rolls in!*

As he came closer a blend of whisky fumes and the sweet sickish odour of cannabis preceded him. Doran pulled him into the house and slammed the front door.

She said, "You have just declared in song that your entire family is engaged in prostitution, illegal liquor distillation and drug peddling. Ogle wants you in the Long Drawing Room with the rest of us, and if you sing any more of that he'll understand it, Welsh or not, and get heavy with you. Now put that thing out, come in, sit next to me and keep quiet. Okay?"

Howell smiled seraphically. She doubted whether he had followed a word of her warning.

They entered the Long Drawing Room amid an almost palpable hush. Ogle fixed them with a piercing eye.

"You're with us, Mr. Evans? *Quite* with us?"

Doran spoke up hastily. "He's sorry, he was trying to get his car out of the snow." She pulled Howell down beside her, hoping that his aura was not reaching as far as Ogle.

Rodney whispered, "Tired and emotional, is he?"

"Stewed, utterly gone. Could be trouble."

Ogle addressed the assembly. "Well, ladies and gentlemen, with the limited machinery at our disposal, we've done our best to unravel the tragic events of the past two days. Never," he burlesqued a Churchillian accent, "has so much been accomplished in so short a time by so few." He looked round for applause.

Rodney groaned softly but audibly to ears as sensitive as Ogle's. "You said something, sir?"

"Me? I? No."

"Well, to recap. Our first query was the identity of the gentleman whose corpse was discovered in the grounds of the kitchen area yesterday morning. Inquiries have now ascertained that he was a Mr. Reginald Haslem, antique dealer of Brighton."

Nobody reacted.

"Inquiries have also ascertained that Mr. Haslem's family can suggest no reason why he should have been killed. His wife informs us that he received a telephone call on the night of the twentieth, after which he told her that he would be attending the Antiques Roadshow at Caxton Manor on the following morning. This did not strike her as in any way abnormal." He cleared his throat, as though to draw attention to his flow of eloquence.

"Yet, ladies and gentlemen, this man was the victim of an apparently motiveless crime. Of murder."

This time he got his reaction. Doran had not passed on the information given to her by Sam: it was none of her business to spread alarm and despondency. Mrs. Blatt squealed, "Oh, Lionel!" and clutched her husband. Sara, Perdita, Tiggy, John and Terry displayed various degrees of surprise and shock. Morven crossed herself—that was the second time Doran had seen her do it. The hectic colour left Dermid's cheeks. Henry's tense expression seemed that of a man who had had as much as he could stand.

Yvonne said, "Oh *no*. Two deaths! It'll ruin the Manor. We'll have to close. Blast."

Speaking for the management, conscientious girl, thought Doran.

"H-how was it done?" Terry asked quaveringly.

"Manual pressure on the neck. Probably by karate methods. Very slight bruising."

"Aeow Gawd!" Watch it, lad, your accent's slipping.

"Well," Ogle continued briskly, "pending further inquiries being made as far as is possible in present conditions, we have the question of Mr. Falk Lydgate, murdered by some person or persons unknown. Now," and his accent also was slipping, for the word came out as Naow, "police interrogation has uncovered no motive for the murder, though it seems quite evident that deceased was not a close friend of any of you."

Nobody commented.

"From examination of deceased the police have arrived at the conclusion that death was brought about by the insertion from the rear of a sharp instrument between the first and second ribs, penetrating top of left lung and causing haemorrhage leading to almost instant death."

Perdita very slowly, very gracefully, keeled over and subsided in a heap on the floor. Her long brown hair spilled out of her cap and spread about her.

A dead mermaid, thought Doran.

In the resultant confusion Howell came out of his semi-coma with a sharp snore and a strangled cry, and Doran took the opportunity of hauling him to his feet and out of the room. He stumbled beside her through the inner hall as she searched for somewhere to leave him safely. One door handle refused to yield to her touch. With a cold frisson she realized that it was the door of the Flower Room.

In the library she pushed him down on the edge of a wing chair. He caught at her hand and began to weep.

"Oh, Howell, don't. Pull yourself together."

"So sorry. So sorry, *merch*. Let you down. Bloody oaf."

"No, you're not. But you're a bloody fool. If only you'd stop taking that—stuff. You do know it'll lead to worse things, don't you? Here, let me have them." She frisked the pockets of his coat and removed a small packet.

"Now. Go and change. Get those frightful boots off and have a bath. You can use my room if you like—Princess Louise." She thrust the key at him. "Make yourself some tea at the same time, and stay there—don't cross Ogle's path again today or he'll get you. At the moment he's too full of his own importance to notice."

Ogle was waiting for her. Perdita had been removed. The formal group of Ogle's audience had been broken up and were obviously hoping to be allowed to leave, but with a papal gesture he detained them.

"Now that Miss—Mrs.—Er is back with us, I can tell you that after a thorough search no such sharp instrument as the one I referred to has been found, and no suspicion attaches to anyone present, or recently removed." This was pointedly addressed to Doran. "With regard to the disappearance of Mrs. Mercia Lang and Mr. Albert Prinn, the police are now conducting a search in the village, beyond which they are unlikely to have gone. Until some trace of them comes to light I needn't ask you to remain within the building. Not difficult, ha ha."

The company thankfully dispersed. His words were lost in the general dispersal. Doran returned to the conservatory, followed by Rodney. He shut the door and leaned against it. They breathed deeply of peace, warmth and the scent of geranium and hyacinth, fern and chrysanthemum. Japonica blossoms, waxy pink, shone among bright green leaves. Forced strawberries were tight green buttons.

"It's men like Ogle who get sermonizing a bad name. But for such as him I could fill the Albert Hall twice nightly."

"Oh, he's a preposterous ass. He used to be rude and brash, now he's turned himself into what he thinks a chief inspector ought to be like. Goodness knows what he's been reading."

"*Boy's Own Paper, 1901.* What's this about your two missing friends?"

"Obviously they haven't got far. Rodney." She picked off a fading hyacinth bell, examining it absently. "Mercia's an Arms and Armour expert. If anyone knew about sharp instruments, she would."

"Also about exactly where to place it in the human anatomy?"

"I can't say. She was frightened of something. Perhaps he threatened her and she went for him with a knife."

"In the back?"

"Well. Not likely, no. And the other man, Haslem, wasn't killed like that. But Mercia might have learned karate for self-defence. She's a little thing, the sort who needs it. She's got a shop, I know, and when one's in a shop alone with valuables one's extremely vulnerable."

"I was aware of that. I wish you'd give yours up."

Doran was not to be diverted. "It's not use talking about that till we know what you're going to be doing. We can't afford to lose one income. Mercia . . . she's just the sort of helpless-looking person who turns out to be a murderer. As for Bert Prinn, I don't think he's got the brains."

"But murderers are notoriously stupid."

"What about the sharp instrument? The police haven't found it, obviously, or Ogle would have been bragging about how he personally spotted it gleaming in an unlikely corner, identified the bloodstains as human, and with the aid of his pocket anatomical chart deduced exactly how it fitted the wound. I suppose they've been through all our rooms."

Rodney toyed with a potting fork in a box of gardening tools. "The sharp instrument could have been something like this. Or merely a knife from the kitchens, where I understand such things are not uncommon—the murderer could simply have borrowed and returned it."

"Of course," Doran replied with sarcasm. "I can just imagine the scene—the murderer lurking round the kitchen door until nobody was in sight, then darting in and replacing it, having washed it under a tap. Or handing it to one of the staff, still somewhat bloody. 'Your steak knife.' 'Oh, thank you, madam, or sir. I hope it came in handy.' This is all getting us nowhere, let's go and see what Howell's doing."

As they left the conservatory Sam was approaching them.

"Someone told me I'd find you in here," he said. "We've found the missing pair—I thought you'd like to know."

"Oh, where, Sam? How did you find them? What did they say?" Doran asked eagerly. Rodney was silent. He had never fancied confrontation with murderers, though it had been forced upon him once or twice. A human soul was something for which he felt responsibility.

Sam told them that it had not been difficult. The four policemen searching the village had found tracks leading to a farm outbuilding which contained three cars as well as a tractor and a small lorry. Among them, huddled in sacks and miscellaneous workers' garments, sat Mercia and Bert, wet, half-frozen, starving and miserable.

"She said, 'We couldn't get any further. I wish to God we'd never tried.' She was crying as if she'd never stop. Mr.

Prinn told us none of the vehicles would start. They'd been eating dried hops and drinking handfuls of melted snow. I don't know when I was sorrier for anybody.''

"Oh, Sam! Poor things. I don't care what they've done.''

"Can we do anything for them?" Rodney asked.

'' 'Fraid not. They're being looked after, fed and given dry clothes, that sort of thing, with Mr. Burnelle in charge.'' He didn't add that Ogle was hovering over the whole operation, vulture-like. "The girls are seeing to Mrs. Lang. She's not very well, it seems, so she'll be staying in bed while her statement's taken. The police surgeon's with her.''

"Poor Mercia. Sam . . . I don't like to ask this, it seems very callous just now—but could you somehow let us know what they say in their statements? It's very unethical, of course, only . . .''

Sam shook his head. "I know you. I'll see what I can do. But I can't promise anything, Doran.''

In his quiet way Sam was very persuasive. Against Ogle's irritable objections he succeeded in sitting in on the recording of statements from Mercia and Bert, with Ride very unobtrusively making a full shorthand version. This was not difficult, with two such distressed and halting speakers. Ride then made a transcription which, a couple of hours later, Sam handed to Doran without comment.

MRS. MERCIA LANG.

"I know we shouldn't have run for it like that, I said to Bert it was silly. Only I was frightened, because the telly's showing that film of the Roadshow tomorrow night and I thought he'd be certain to see it and know where I was. It's my husband, you see, he works down here. We're separated and I'm living with someone else and he's still very mad about it. He lost track of me when I took over the shop I've got now and called it by a trade name, but I knew they'd give my name away on telly when they showed a close-up of me. I told them not to do that, but they did.

"He said he'd kill me, me and the children and the guy I'm living with, if he ever got at us, and he meant it, he's very violent when he's drunk. Yes, he does drink an awful lot. If he'd traced me here he'd have got my address out of the organizers. Yes, I know I was taking a risk coming here, but it was the first time I'd been asked to do anything like that and I suppose I was flattered.

"I wouldn't have done if it I'd thought more. It was just that when I got here I saw a map and realized how near it was to where he works. I told Bert about it and he was very nice because he was in a mess himself. When the snow came it took a load off my mind, knowing my husband couldn't get at me till it cleared.

"We'd seen a weather forecast saying there'd only be another day or so of it before people would be able to move about again. So when Bert said he was going to make a run for it I thought I'd have a go too. Ought to have known it was no good. But I'd phoned the kids and after that I was sort of desperate.

"Yes, I did know Bert before, we'd met once or twice in the way of business. But I didn't know Mr. Lydgate at all. Of course I hadn't got anything against him, how could I have? He thought I was a silly bitch, I could tell that, and I thought he was a stuffy old queen, that's all there was to it.

"No, I've never used a dagger on anyone in my life." (Pause for sobbing.) "The very idea . . . Daggers and swords and things are what I deal in and I know a lot about them, but I hate violence. I can't talk any more . . ."

Here the transcript ended.

"Oh," said Doran. "Oh, poor creature. We never thought of that."

Bert Prinn's statement was shorter.

"I don't know what Mercia's told you but she's absolutely in the clear about what's happened here. We didn't know

156

Lydgate was dead, even. We were probably away from here before it happened.

"I wanted to get away because my wife had been threatening to leave me. She's got a boyfriend, he's always been after her and I know he's told her things like he wants to take her away and our two kids. She gets a bit bored with me, you see, she's very pretty and she likes a lot of social life, and she isn't interested in antiques. I was going to do something about it, move to a new house, back where we used to live, where she's got friends.

"I thought if I was away from home long he'd come blarneying round her, perhaps get her to go off with him." (Emotional interlude.) "I knew he'd be no good to her, and he didn't even like kids, I could tell that. He used to call me a name I don't let anyone call me. No, I'm not saying what it is.

"So when the phones went dead and I couldn't get through to her I panicked. Then when I did get through there was no answer. I thought it had happened, she'd gone, and I went nearly mad.

"No, I didn't ring the neighbours, I hadn't that much sense. I thought I'd try to get home, get a lift to London and catch a train, because they said it was almost clear of snow up there. We, Mercia and me, found some sticks and a shovel lying about, that we thought would help us get to the village now that the drive's been cleared. But it was a hell of a job. And then when we got to the farm I couldn't get any of the cars or the tractor to start, and we'd no money to offer anyone, not to speak of.

"Mercia's not to blame for any of it, it's me that's been the bloody fool.

"No, I didn't know Lydgate before. Not in my league, or I wasn't in his. I don't think he even noticed me."

* * *

"*He* feels like a bloody fool? What about me?" said Doran. "Remind me to have my imagination removed sometime, will you?"

Rodney said that he would.

"And after all that, it was just a domestic difference, in both cases."

"Domestic differences can be very serious."

"Yes."

"Don't let's forget that."

"I won't. Oh, I won't. I don't suppose they'll be charged with anything worse than wasting police time, will they?"

"I doubt it," said Rodney. "By the way, what do you suppose this name was that Prinn's rival called him, so unforgivably?"

Doran told him about Ethelbert.

"Oh. Oh dear, poor chap. I suppose one shouldn't laugh." But he did.

Chapter 11

Horrid Warning

Two of the suspects were out of the running. That left only three, for it was impossible to consider seriously any of the young staff as a murderer, or the Blatts or Mrs. Rapton.

Doran found that she was very unwilling to think that either Morven, Dermid or Henry had deliberately killed two people. But, whoever had, it was not a practice to be encouraged, and murderers were notable for letting one successful murder lead to another.

There was no logical reason why she should take it upon herself to solve the crimes. That was what the police were there for. But Ogle had taken over the police operation, and he was blinded by self-love, not to be trusted to follow any line which didn't lead to his own glorification. He had got on in his career largely by bluffing people: but he would not bluff Doran. There was a personal antagonism between them.

"I must just go and check up on Howell," she told Rodney.

"Do that." He wandered off to the library, where Terry had now lit a fire, and settled beside it with a pile of books and Briar the labrador, who instantly claimed him as a long-lost friend and rolled lovingly on his feet until he put them up on a footstool.

Howell was awake, sober, and penitent. He had taken advantage of Doran's shower, which was now in a very wet and untidy state, and had shaved with Rodney's razor. This had improved his appearance, but not the razor's. She set herself resignedly to clear up the mess.

"Stopped snowing, it has," he said. "Shall I try and dig Harris out for you?"

"That would be very kind, Howell." It would also keep him busy and out of trouble, not to mention removing him from beneath the official gaze. "Just before you go—which of our dealer pals in Eastgate do you think would be the best source of information—about other dealers?"

Howell pondered. "Art Hidley's got a lot of contacts in London."

"I don't want to know about London, and I can't stand Art Hidley."

"Well, then. What about Meg? She spreads her net wide, you'd be surprised, though she does go for a lot of old-clo' tat."

"Yes, I know." Doran smiled reminiscently. "She found me my wedding dress in some theatre collection. Of course, she gets around, because she drives and Peg doesn't."

Meg and Peg were a married couple, neighbours of Howell's, an odd but amiable enough pair. Doran had discovered (because she couldn't bear not to know) that Peg's nickname, unsuitable to a man who sported a naval beard and dressed like a Victorian sailor, came from the fact that his parents had christened him Peggotty—presumably in a burst of Dickensian enthusiasm. Meg was tiny, vague, and dressed in a curious selection of garments of several periods and mixed ethnic origins from her wardrobe stock.

"Right," Doran said. "Good idea. Off you go, then. Quick."

Off he went, quick, as meek as a lamb. She would make something of him yet.

She settled in the crinoline chair at the bedside and picked up the telephone, a streamline instrument. The Manor would never descend to the vulgarity of a tarty imitation of a 1920s

Ericsson model. Yvonne, on the switchboard, seemed surprised but grateful to be asked for an outside number.

"Meg? Oh, Peg. Is she around?"

"That you, Doran? I'll get her. Filthy weather. Hang on."

Meg came on the line, breathy and fluting. "Doran? Darling, pet. Kiss kiss. How amazing to hear a human voice—my dear, we're snowed under, literally, the stuff's as high as the parlour window and coming in through the attic ceiling, Peg's got a bucket under it. How are you doing at Abbotsbourne? Oh, but of course you're not there, you're at the Roadshow at Whatsit Manor."

Doran gave Meg a very brief rundown on the situation at the Manor.

"Darling, I *know*, it was on the news, about the Roadshow being stopped by the snow and a man's body found—one of the punters, was it? How awful for you, but no, of course you'd enjoy it, if you know what I mean, you do like getting mixed up in things. I'm glad it wasn't me. I'd have swooned away, but then I don't suppose you saw it . . ."

"As a matter of fact I found it. And no, I didn't enjoy it all that much. Meg, do you know a man called Reg Haslem—Brighton, Thornhill Street, only deals with the Trade?"

Meg's voice rose to a bat's squeak. "But of course I do! I've known him for years. Don't tell me it was him?"

"Yes, it was. The police didn't want his name broadcast until relatives had been informed, as they say. Do you, by any chance, know what his particular line was, if he had one—or whether he was into anything in the least bit dicey?"

There was an un-Meglike pause at the other end of the line, and her voice, when it spoke, was faintly hesitant. "He did a lot with rather grand jewellery. Export stuff, that sort of thing. And he got things for big collectors, people who'd pay twice round the earth for a teentsy little bit of Fabergé."

"They'd be lucky to find one."

"They would, wouldn't they? Oh gosh, someone's just

fallen over in the road—I'll give Peg a call, it's a poor old man and he can't get up by himself—Peg!''

Doran waited until dialogue had been exchanged. She was sorry about the poor old man but his plight was not going to keep her from her purpose. ''Meg,'' she said firmly when a door had been heard to shut, ''I know we don't tell on each other, whatever we know, but I'm asking about Reg Haslem for a very good reason. It's bound to come out sooner or later'' (lies, lies) ''and I need to know now, at once, to get somebody out of a very awkward spot.'' Or into one. ''I promise I won't use any information you give me unless I have to. Do you know anything Reg Haslem handled that could have . . . got him into trouble?''

''Well. I shouldn't tell you. But—you know when people own jewellery that's too valuable to wear, and costs too much to insure? They often get it replaced by synthetics, shove it in a bank and keep stumm about it.''

''I thought they only did that in old, old whodunits.''

''Well, they still do. Reg sometimes handles that sort of thing, taking a big cut.'' She giggled. ''He told me about it once—he rather fancied me, you know. About the synthetics—emeralds and sapphires and rubies—did you know red spinel looks exactly like real ruby?—and of course pearls. They can fake those so that only a very, very special specialist can tell them from the real thing.''

Doran asked carefully, ''Does—did Reg do antique pieces?''

''Art Nouveau, dogs of Fo, Bonaparte bees? Oh yes. Only he didn't *do* them, he got them done.''

''Where?''

Pause. ''I don't think I ought to say. Though they're quite sound as a firm, I'm sure, perfectly okay. Only if anything got out about some pieces that hadn't been, well, *right*, I might find myself getting a solicitor's letter. Or you might. So.''

"I'll take the risk—and I promise your name won't come into it at all, Meg. Just tell me."

A sigh. "All right. Mackie and Steinmann."

There was more chat, but not much, for Meg was unusually anxious to get off the line. She wouldn't admit to knowing the address or even locality of the firm. What amazing luck, that she had known Haslem. But then one could never tell with people, they were such caves of mystery, full of treasure or rubbish or secrets. Doran went down to Reception and gleaned from the London telephone directories.

"I'm going to make a few calls," she told Yvonne. "I hope it won't keep you from anything you should be doing." The desk was invisible for piles of paper and the word-processor on the table beside it was diligently printing out. Yvonne was making up for time lost in attending to guests. She smiled frostily, her fingers hovering over her calculator. "Go ahead, madam. I'll put it all on the bill. But you won't find many people in their offices."

She was right. Switchboards were unmanned or answered by machines, staff were off with flu or had (ridiculously) gone skiing. The snow might be lighter in London, but it was having its effect. Of those human voices which answered, some had colds, others bad tempers, and there was a general consensus of agreement among them not to tell Doran what she wanted to know.

Over an hour later she found it out. In the conurbation of industrial areas south-east of Glasgow was situated the firm of Mackie and Steinmann.

Mackie and Steinmann were at home, so to speak. The Scottish voice on their switchboard glacially refused to pass Doran on to anyone else in the firm. They were all "away", in any case, which Doran correctly took to mean in Scots parlance that they had gone home.

* * *

163

Rodney closed his book resignedly. He had been left peacefully alone by the glowing fire, Briar snoring gently at his feet, and here was Doran back, incandescent with excitement. He looked at his watch: good gracious, it was after six.

She glanced round the inner hall conspiratorially. There was no sign of life, apart from themselves. She pulled up a chair close to his and talked rapidly in an undertone.

"But," he said, "all this is pure speculation. Why should Morven be mixed up with a gem-faking firm, just because it's based in Scotland? And what if she did fake the second-sight thing about the Jewel? Natural enough, wanting to impress a captive audience. Doesn't necessarily mean that she faked the thing itself."

"Why did she go to all the trouble of looking up King Alfred in the library? It sounded so convincing, but it was just a crib. And when I overheard Dermid telling her it was faked she didn't deny it."

"You mean you weren't eavesdropping long enough to hear her deny it."

"If you like to put it so rudely. No, she planted that object, which is why the man who brought it hasn't got in touch. He never will, either, he'll just melt away. And Lydgate knew it had been planted, and what it was. Rodney! He was telephoning, the night we were shown the Jewel. What if he were calling somebody who'd back him up, somebody who knew the truth?"

"What if he wasn't? A man can telephone from an hotel without being mixed up in stratagems and spoils."

Doran brushed this truism aside. "That Latin quote of his about serpents in bosoms and deceiving the public was directed at Morven—I'm sure of that now."

"Hmm. It could have been directed at anybody—and it was your friend Henry who produced the fake jewel. Just because the lady and the firm are both Scottish—a bit thin, don't you think?"

"That's not all. I know what the weapon was, you see. Obviously the police couldn't find one in any of our rooms—none of us has brought much luggage, and it isn't the sort of house that has an armoury draped all over the walls. But . . ."

Sounds of arrival and conversation came from the main hall. Doran recognized the shrillish voice of Miss Pell, the Roadshow organizer, talking to Terry, who seemed to be calming her. In a moment she was with them, no longer boiler-suited, huddled in winter gear. She hurried to the fire and held out her hands to it.

"My God, am I glad to see a proper fire! I can't tell you what's it's been like, getting here from my friend's cottage—she lives just outside the village and the road's still blocked . . ."

Doran interrupted. "I'm sure you'd love a drink, Miss Pell. Terry, will you get drinks for all of us, there's a nice boy?"

Over the drinks Miss Pell shed her top layer of garments and sat down, as Doran had hoped she would do. Her tale of snow horrors was prodigious. She had no idea who Rodney was, cared not at all, but deluged them with what might well be an unending saga of snow, ice, falls, helpful strangers and her own sufferings, now being modified by rum and Coke.

"You see, I felt I *had* to get back, even though the Roadshow had been cancelled after one day, because it *was* my responsibility and my firm would expect me to know exactly what happened . . . if you could tell me, Miss Fairweather?"

Doran took a deep breath and launched into her prepared inquisition.

"Certainly, I'll tell you anything you like—but first, please could you tell me one or two things? Just for my own information, so that I shall know in future how to get on another of these gigs. For instance, where does Mrs. Cair live?"

Miss Pell looked nonplussed. "I don't see . . . well, she has a flat in London, but I believe her shop is on the outskirts of Edinburgh."

"Quite a way from here. How did your firm come to invite her so far south?"

"Mr. Gore recommended her. They're friends, I believe. Of course, we know him very well. He said she was excellent, especially on jewellery."

"Did she know what other experts would be attending?"

"Yes, of course. I always send out lists when I get the acceptances. Naturally people want to know who else would be taking part. I don't see why you're interested in all this, Miss Fairweather."

"It's immensely helpful. Do tell me, now—who selected Mr. Scance?"

"The firm did. We had to have a clocks and watches person, and we knew how dedicated he was, though we were a bit worried when he was so ill."

"Ah, yes." Doran's tone was casual. "What was the matter with him, by the way?"

Miss Pell bridled. "I really don't see what that can possibly have to do with you. Nothing infectious, I can assure you, in case you're worried." She collected an armful of wraps and scarves.

"My wife," said Rodney gently, "has a very particular reason for wanting to know, or she wouldn't ask you about anything so personal. I can promise you it will be completely confidential."

It was the voice of authority. Miss Pell recognized it, as though he were wearing the dog collar he had left at home. Meekly she answered, "I believe it was a form of kidney failure. Very nasty, but they got it in time, he just has to be careful what he eats and drinks."

"Yes, I'd noticed," Doran said. "It's really most kind of you to answer all these questions. Most useful. Now oughtn't you to run along and change and get really warm?"

Miss Pell went, not exactly running. As she walked upstairs, burdened, her thoughts were almost visible through the back of her wild-haired head. What an extraordinary young woman: how could all that information be useful to her, and why hadn't she asked the experts herself? And that man, with the beautiful voice, saying "my wife," about Miss Fairweather? What could it all mean?

Her slow-moving form disappeared round the corner of the stairs.

"Well," said Doran, carefully putting another log on the fire. "Kidney trouble. How very unromantic."

"So much for Keats."

"I might have known, no alcohol and low-protein sandwiches. Oh, well, at least Dermid's not dying. But my other theories—nothing wrong with them, is there? Morven knew that Lydgate would be here, and *he* knew that *she* would. And it was Henry . . ." She paused, thinking, realizing.

"It was your friend Henry who got her here."

"Not Dermid. But Henry told me that he drove them both down, as though he'd quite casually picked them up. That wasn't true."

"It is a flaw," Rodney said, as though to himself, *"in happiness, to see beyond our bourn—It forces us in summer skies to mourn, It spoils the singing of the Nightingale."*

Doran came out of the abstraction which had kept her eyes on the flames and her lips in a sad droop. "It wasn't happiness. It was . . . I don't know what. A compensation for missing you, I suppose. And . . . well, I always had an eye for a pretty fellow. After all, that's why I picked you."

"Oh, was that it? I thought it was for the beauty of my nature and the fact that I cost little to feed. And at least I haven't got white hair. Meow."

Doran ignored the jibe. "Well, I shall go on deducing. And I shan't tell you any more at the moment, if you don't mind."

"I don't mind, my darling." He didn't mind. His instinct

told him that there was still something to find out at the Manor, and that Doran was the person to do it.

She lingered. She had not gone far enough in justifying Henry's attraction for her, and it wasn't easy to find the right words.

"He, er, Henry, sort of thinks on my lines. Our lines. Capping quotes . . . and so on."

"Oh, yes?" Rodney's tone was icy. She had said exactly the wrong thing.

The now-familiar buffet supper was eaten in the dining room, since the Long Drawing Room was beginning to show signs of wear and tear in the form of glass-rings on polished furniture and bits of tomato and prawn embedded in a century-old Aubusson carpet. John arrived with fresh coffee and the news that a thaw had set in, very light rain was falling, melting the snow.

"Looks as if we might be on the move by morning."

Mrs. Blatt clutched her husband's arm. "Oh Lionel! Home for lunch!"

"Thank God," Sara said to Perdita. "They'll be able to take that—body—away, and Mrs. Rapton can calm down, poor old duck."

Doran went over to them. "No thanks, I've had enough to eat. Tell me something. The night Mr. Lydgate was killed, I met you, Perdita, coming out of my room just before I went to bed. You'd been making up my fire, very kindly. Did you go straight to bed yourself, or did you come down the staff staircase again for anything?"

Perdita stretched her baby-blue eyes. "No, madam. I remembering talking to you, and you told me to put an extra blanket on my bed. I did, and I went straight off."

"Right. And you, Sara—did you come down again?"

Sara shook her head. "I was nearly asleep when Perdita came up."

"Thank you, both of you. Don't mention that I asked

you.'' She moved to where Tiggy was pouring coffee, detached her from John's side, and asked her the same question.

''No. I'd had a bath and I was flat out. Acksherly I didn't even hang my uniform up, and we're supposed to do that, every night, because some of them are real, *totally* Edwardian—mine is, it's got a taffeta skirt.''

''Where are the other uniforms kept?''

Tiggy looked surprised, as if everyone ought to know. ''In the big wardrobe cupboard at the bottom of the staff stairs, on the Bachelor Gents' landing, acksherly, next to Beau Nash.''

Doran thanked her. On the Bachelor Gents' landing, at the end of which a sharp right turn led to a long window. A window which had been wide open, that night. Anybody seeing a woman in a black skirt and white pinafore up there would have thought nothing of it. She had thought nothing of it herself until much later.

Morven, Dermid and Henry sat together on a sofa. Dermid's arm lay along the top of it, just not resting on Morven's shoulders. His fine aquiline profile was turned towards her, rapt. Henry seemed lost in thought, chasing a crumb round a plate with his fork.

Howell, who had charmed a plate of cold sausages out of one of the girls, was eating his way through it. ''Starvin', I am,'' he told Doran almost unintelligibly, ''after all that slog. Got Harris almost clear, though. You can get the passenger door open now, if you . . . here, you all right?''

''Perfectly. Why?''

''You got a funny look, that's all.'' He stared after her, sausage pensively poised.

The police were in a group by themselves, perched on easy chairs and sofas. None of them looked as if they were there for choice. Burnelle was thinking of the other things he ought to be doing with his time, Ogle had tried and failed to chat up the three girls and Yvonne (who had rebuffed him in no uncertain terms—how did she come to know such expressions? His mother in Beckenham would have called her unladylike.) The young men were playing cards and keeping a low profile. And Sam Eastry was restless, frequently going to a window to draw back the curtain and watch the weather.

Rodney, too, was restless, indeed nervous. The long gracious room was too still. People were talking, when they talked at all, too quietly.

Was it, he wondered, that in a sense they were in the presence of death? A dead man lay in the Flower Room, unavenged. Did such blood cry out, disturbing the peace of the living? He rather thought it might.

Suddenly too oppressed to sit still, he uncoiled himself from the deep couch. "I'm going upstairs to telephone home."

Doran nodded. She, too, would have to face up to the realities of home, when this macabre interlude was over. She gave him five minutes, then followed him.

The other end of the telephone conversation was perfectly audible, for the speaker was Vi Small, whose voice inclined more to the duck than the dove.

Rodney was saying, "But I don't understand why Carole isn't there."

"Because she went off when she shouldn't have, that's why. My friend Hayley just happened to see her when she went over to see her old mum, I mean Hayley's old mum, being that Meals on Wheels can't get round in this weather and her mum's ever so frail . . ."

"Yes, yes. But why did Carole go home? She was supposed to be sleeping at Bell House."

"Well, I did just knock at her door and ask, seeing I thought it was funny myself, and she said her hubby had phoned to say their youngest was running a temp. So she thought she'd go and see to him, and come back tonight, only she hasn't. Oh, and she borrowed Miss Doran's wellies, so as not to spoil them silly pink boots of hers. So, not wanting to think of Helena all by herself, I come over and a good thing I did, poor kid, seeing she doesn't seem at all well. And here I am still waiting for Carole." Her tone was triumphant, she had found her young rival out in a fault. "She won't get back tonight, if I know her, it's thawing and ever so slippy."

Doran advanced. "Let me talk to Vi."

Rodney shook his head at her. "It's very good of you, Vi. Are you saying that Helena's been on her own, and that she's not well?"

"That's right. Very quiet, not a bit like herself. She's here, if you want a word with her."

"Please."

Helena's speech was not clearly audible at second hand. Rodney's expression was puzzled. "Speak up," he said, "I can't hear you. I'm sorry about you being alone in the house. Is your back giving trouble again? What? *Who?* Oh, yes, I think you did mention something . . . *Do* you?"

He turned to Doran. "She wants to speak to you." He might have been announcing a call from the Queen, by his awestruck tone.

"Hello, Helena."

"Are you all right?" The tone was soft, diffident.

"*Me?* Yes, I'm fine. Are you? That's more the question. I'm sorry about Carole going off like that."

"It didn't matter. I've been doing some homework. And tidying up my room—you'll be pleased when you see it."

"Yes, I'm sure I shall. Er—you haven't let Tybalt into the drawing room again, have you? Because . . ."

"No, he followed me into the kitchen and we stayed there, it was warmer. And do you know, he sat on my lap. I've got to go now, Vi wants to talk again."

Doran hung up after some domestic details had been discussed.

171

"What on earth . . . ?" she said. "That didn't sound like Helena at all."

"I know. But it was. Incredibly."

"But why? I mean, homework, tidying, Tybalt-nursing . . . I should have thought she'd be frantic by now, left alone like that, and Tybalt ripping up the best carpets like a mad puma. And her voice sounds funny. She must be sickening for something, that's what it is. Vi said Carole's young Kevin has got the bug. Oh dear." Either that, Doran thought, or Helena's done something so awful that it's knocked the fight out of her, seeing the ruin.

"She said something to me about Annabella—that's her friend, isn't it, the superannuated sixteen-year-old? I didn't understand what she meant. You're probably right, she's picked up something at school and isn't quite herself." He had wandered near the door of their bathroom. Suddenly he pointed dramatically.

"My razor! *Which of you have done this?*"

"Oh. Oh mercy. Don't look at me, I haven't started shaving—it was Howell, making himself look respectable. I thought I'd dealt with it but I obviously haven't. I'll do it now."

"No, no, pray don't trouble. I can clean it up myself, or not clean it up and grow a beard. Come to think of it, about time I transformed myself into a patriarch. If you know what I mean."

"Yes . . . It will be curious living with Isaiah, or whoever is the patriarch of your choice. Obadiah, Micah, Nahum?"

"Or even Habakkuk or Zephaniah, who knows? Where are you going?"

"To see Harris. Howell's been very kindly working on him, digging him out. If the roads are clearish tomorrow I want to be able to start him up."

* * *

172

In the porch she found several pairs of wellingtons, evidently left thoughtfully there for anyone who wanted to go out. She chose a pair which fitted her approximately.

Conditions outside had changed dramatically. Thaw had indeed set in, bringing a rawer quality of cold with it, and turning the trodden snow into a muddy slush. Everything dripped. From the portico and roof of the Manor lumps of melted snow fell in blobs, one of them landing neatly between Doran's coat-hood and her neck. Cursing it, she plodded round the corner of the house to where Harris stood, no longer a shapeless white heap but his usual self of metallic gold, a car among other cars which were turning back into their own likenesses, like Circe's swine released from the spell.

Last time she had been in that place she had fallen over the corpse of Reg Haslem. "Little did I think . . ." she murmured, mocking herself. "Had I but known. Ah, well, normality returns at last." But for one situation with which she must deal.

She thought about that, as she unlocked the car, mopped up with a duster the moisture which had seeped in from the heavy snow piled on it. Its interior was dankly uninviting. She got out and inspected the ground, easy enough to see by the standard lamps in the drive and the light above the door to the kitchens. It was a swamp, but she thought, a negotiable swamp. Harris was youngish and powerful, his tyres new.

The engine, bitterly cold, was so slow in starting that she was sure the battery was dead. Then, to her pleased surprise, a faint shudder within the bonnet gave way to a steady throb. Harris rides again, bless him.

The area behind the car was clear. With jerks, futile chuggings, and oaths, Doran finally persuaded Harris to move back a few inches, then a few more. Some diligent hacking at the slush with the spade which Howell had carelessly but fortuitously left propped against the next car cleared enough space for Harris to be backed sufficiently to be driven out. It was, in aeronautical terms, a bumpy ride, very hard on the driver's wrists and arms, and painfully slow. It was half an hour before she could manoeuvre Harris down the slight slope of concrete on the tarmac drive, now comparatively clear.

Above her, the Triceratops hung his head dejectedly. Perhaps he had enjoyed his night and day of glory, clearing a road to civilization for his masters, and was now suffering withdrawal symptoms. She drove Harris slowly, past him, across the uneven surface, to the end of the drive, where she stopped, positioned conveniently for the carriage road that led to the village. No sheep were to be seen: that was a relief, to know that they had not frozen.

On the coach house a clock chimed, startling the silence. Ten strokes.

The time had fled unnoticed, and the thing she still had to deal with had gone from her mind temporarily. Now, hot from exertion, wet and uncomfortable, she wondered whether, after all, the idea which had come to her after supper, watching Dermid, was not the wildest speculation even she had ever imagined. But there had been the look on his face, that afternoon: the Glory and the Dream.

Yes, she would do something about it. She kicked off the boots and left her damp coat in the hall.

The Drawing Room was deserted but for Sara and Tiggy tidying away. It was probably too late; she could hardly follow Dermid to his bedroom. If he was in it . . .

The door of the library was open, the lights on.

And luck, or a benevolent fate, had directed her rightly. He was there, searching through a shelf. The dogs lay on the hearthrug. As Doran entered they wagged their tails, smiling in their sleep.

"Ah," said Dermid. "Doran. You haven't got Keats, by any chance? We were talking about him the other night, and I can't find him."

"Yes, as a matter of fact I have got him up in my room."

Now, seeing Dermid, she knew she was right. A serenity of anticipatory joy bathed him like a light. It was her task to put out that light, to be cruel yet kind. *And shall I see thee made a serpent's prey?*

"I could probably tell you exactly which poem you're looking for," she said in a rush.

He smiled. "I doubt that very much."

"But I could, you know. *The Eve of St. Agnes. Into her dream he melted, as the rose Blendeth its odour with the violet.* Right?"

The high colour stood out on his cheekbones brilliantly, then faded. Rose, hearing her name, raised her head from the hearthrug. A log shifted and fell, sending up a flame.

"How did you know?" Dermid asked.

"The consummation of Porphyro's longing for Madeline. That's what you've been promised, isn't it? In return for silence about the Saxon Jewel. She's waiting for you now. Don't go to her, Dermid. She's not what she seems, she's a murderess. I hate telling you this but I have to. If you go to her room now you won't come out alive."

He was holding on to the bookcase, white-faced and trembling. Doran took his arm and led him a few steps to a chair. "There. Sit down. Breathe deeply, that's right."

She moved away from him to the door. Rose suddenly left the hearthrug and came to her side, looking up inquiringly.

"Good girl," Doran said. "It's all right, stay with Briar and take care of poor Dermid."

But Rose was already through the door. Doran followed her, key in hand, shut the door and locked it from the outside.

Rose was halfway up the staircase, looking back, beckoning her on, bright-eyed, a dog who has found a pheasant for its master to retrieve.

Chapter 12

What wreath for Lamia?

Morven had been waiting for the knock at her door. For a moment she stood there, radiant, welcoming, a vision shimmering in a long shining robe which moved from blues to green through all their spectra, turquoise, sage, azure, indigo, peacock, violet, emerald, all changing and glittering as she breathed. *She was a gordian shape of dazzling hue.* She was Lamia.

Then she recognized Doran. The face altered, seemed to stiffen. The bright eyes were glassed over. In the left one the cast appeared, more strongly than Doran had seen it, a disfigurement, not an attraction.

"What do you want?"

Doran went past her, shutting the door and standing against it. The bitch Rose, outside, whined once.

"I just came to tell you not to expect your next victim."

"I'm afraid I don't understand."

"Oh, I think so. Don't tell me I've over-rated your famous intelligence. You've killed two men already, haven't you?" Doran was surprised and pained to notice how fast her heart was beating, when she had hoped to be either completely cool or bold with adrenalin. Her knees were beginning to shake. But Morven had sunk down on the dressing stool, where she sat draped in a classically graceful position, half-leaning against the dressing table, the long legs crossed at

176

the ankles, the shining gown clinging to them, giving the slightest suggestion of a tail.

"Do go on," Morven said pleasantly.

"Reg Haslem was sent for, wasn't he—by Lydgate, who must have known about your connection with him, to give you away about that Saxon jewel. Not that it was any more Saxon than I am, probably less. But you spotted Haslem and persuaded him to step outside with you, and killed him, very cleverly, so that it didn't show. What was it—manual pressure on the neck—the carotids?"

"Did the police tell you that? How clever of them to find out. Yes. I learned the art of karate before I opened the shop— one has to be so careful. But then you know that." She spread her hands, showing them off: such small, creamy, dimpled hands. But there was nothing fragile about them, they were strong, rock-solid; Doran had thought them very like the pretty porcelain hands modelled to hold a small lotus-shaped vase. Sometimes the hand wore a wedding ring and ended at the wrist in a lacy frill or a twist of pearls.

There was a superstition about them in the Trade, held by people who believed that they had been modelled from the hand of the Marquise de Brinvilliers, that charming little multi-poisoner who had paid for her crimes in torture and death on the scaffold. It had lain in some recess of Doran's mind since her first sight of Morven's hands.

Doran tore her gaze away from them, aware that the slow sweet voice was saying, "Tell me more."

"Well. Haslem knew you'd had the jewel faked at the Scottish factory he sometimes dealt with. He was prepared to shop you, and Lydgate wanted you shown up before us all. Why, by the way?"

Morven admired the gleaming shelly nails of her left hand.

"Jealousy, my dear. Did you not deduce that?"

Doran shook her head.

Morven sighed lightly. "Ah, well. I had stolen my husband from him, you see. I was a very innocent creature in those days, and I thought I could get away with it. But they never change (as you might remember if you're thinking of reforming that stupid Welsh terrior of yours). I thought it had worked, but I didn't know my man. Or men. Until Falk stole Angus back, that is. It was a very, very clever seduction. But Falk never forgave me, even though he'd won. He loathed women, and me most of all.

"And I never forgave him. So I killed him. He was going to give me away himself, and in any case it was a pleasure."

Doran's mouth had gone dry, making it difficult to speak. But she must find out the truth. "Why didn't you use karate again?"

"Too cliché, my dear. Besides, I felt the other way would be more artistic—blood on the snow. It was quite easy to get him to that most conveniently remote landing. I called him outside his room—the Beau Nash room. I said he was needed to deal with something. I disguised my voice, of course: I can do a very credible English accent. He came out, followed me towards the open window, and—that was it. Simple."

"I suppose in that dim light he didn't recognize you dressed as a maid. Because you'd borrowed one of the uniforms from their cupboard, hadn't you? And the police couldn't find the sharp instrument because it was fastening your kilt. The *skean-dhu* was a real weapon, not an ornament."

"How clever of you to notice that. My bonnie wee knife. *The bloody Highland blade.* Can you tell me who wrote that, clever Miss Fairweather?"

Doran made an immense effort. "Scott. I think it's *Marmion*, but I'm not sure."

Morven laughed softly. "Not bad for a Sassenach. In fact, *The Last Minstrel*."

"I used to read a lot of Sir Walter." Doran was gabbling, playing for time. "I found him very soothing. So melodious,

178

so, er . . . the last voice of Scottish chivalry, wouldn't you say?'' (Oh, what rubbish.)

"If you say so. I've not met with a lot of Scottish chivalry—or English either, come to that.'' She picked up the silver dagger from where it lay on the dressing table: among, Doran noticed, manicure equipment and a bottle of fine scent, but no cosmetics. So that perfect complexion was all Morven's own.

She toyed with the *skean-dhu*, watching the blade shine and flash in the soft lamp-light. Doran was tensed as a bowstring, waiting for the attack. Had that blade been reddened at Culloden? The dagger was old enough, though newer than the treacherous massacre of Glencoe.

Yet it lay in the hands of a Campbell. What chance would she have if that lithe figure rose, swooped on her?

"I expect,'' said Morven, "that you thought it a shade brutal to throw Falk's body out into the snow. But that was because he had thrown me into the cold. It is very cold, you know, living without love.''

"Yes, I know. And I didn't think it was particularly brutal—rather artistic, really.'' (One should always flatter murderers.) "I did wonder why you bothered to have that jewel made. It must have been a—a very expensive bit of craftsmanship, and it would have been found out sooner or later—probably sooner.''

Morven shrugged. "I had a buyer for it. A simple creature, very rich. With what he paid me I could have bought luxury, things to fill the emptiness. Henry would have taken nothing for himself.''

Things were clicking into place in Doran's mind. "Henry. Henry *knew* about the fake?''

A beautiful smile. "Henry arranged the whole thing. Useful Oxford connections. He had blow-ups done of the Alfred Jewel and gave them to a top artist to copy and change. He

179

had it with him all the time. There was no man who came to the Roadshow and failed to come back. So clever.''

"But—why? What would he get out of it?''

"Me,'' said Morven simply. "I was to be his reward. The most collectable of objects, to Henry, though hardly an antiquity. Dermid would not have known. But then he was foolish enough to look too closely at the jewel. So Dermid will have to die, in case honesty overcomes him at some stage. He is dying in any case, poor bairn.''

"No, he isn't! He's getting over something rather nasty, that's all.'' Doran knew she should keep quiet, but impulse drove her on. "You were going to kill him as you did Haslem, weren't you?''

Morven looked down at her hands, then laid aside the *skean-dhu*.

"He'll know nothing, and die happy.'' She glanced at the bed. "Swoon to death, as your friend Keats puts it. A perfect ending. My loveliness and the hour of his death. Keats again.''

Doran made up her mind to risk everything on one hazardous throw. "Dermid won't be coming to you. I locked him in the library. Try to pull yourself together and face facts, Morven. You can't win . . .''

The tall lithe figure was on its feet, almost touching her, pressing her against the door, the perfect hands moving up to her neck.

"Ah, yes, I can,'' said the perfect lips. There was one desperate chance, and Doran took it, hooking one foot behind Morven's opposite ankle in the backheel which was the only move in wrestling she knew. Miraculously it worked, Morven toppling backwards with Doran in a heap on top of her. At the same time the door burst open and lot of noise, shouting and barking broke out.

Morven rolled away from her attacker and was on her feet in a flash, shrieking as a furry golden thing launched itself

180

at her, and Rose, the gentle Rose, sank her teeth in Morven's leg.

For a second the whole scene froze before Doran's eyes. The glittering figure in its blue-green serpent scales, the beautiful features contorted in pain, the agitated faces and shouting mouths of three men, Henry, Dermid, Rodney, the leaping, barking dog and herself, crouching on the floor in an attitude something like that of the Dying Gladiator.

The picture shattered as Morven sprang forward and pushed the men aside, thrusting through them into the corridor. Somebody reeled and fell—Dermid. Rodney dropped to his knees beside Doran. "Are you all right? Did she hurt you?"

"I'm fine," she gasped. "Never mind me, go after her."

'If you're sure . . .'' He ran off down the corridor, following a trail of blood. Henry stood in the doorway, staring after him, expressionless.

Doran climbed painfully to her feet, clutching her right shoulder, which seemed to be dislocated. Rose jumped up to lick her face.

"Good girl," said Doran, "don't. Sit, will you? Sit. And thank you for what you did. *Very* good dog. They say dogs and children always know," she told Henry, laughing in a way which even to her ears sounded hysterical.

He ignored her. He and Dermid were facing each other, both pale, both stricken, like two duellists who have fired fatal shots at the same time. Dermid got to his feet, moving as stiffly as an old man, and lowered himself to the bed he should have shared with his lady that night.

"She betrayed me," Henry said. "And you. She sold us both down the river." If stone could speak it would have spoken with such a voice.

Dermid nodded slowly. He looked to be on the verge of tears.

"She was going to kill you, Dermid," Doran said.

181

"Treachery and murder. She was a Campbell, you know. One more death would mean nothing to her. The Campbells murdered thirty Macdonalds in the Glen of Weeping that night—people who'd been their hosts for two weeks."

Henry looked at her for the first time. "Doran," he said wearily, "we do know about your great erudition and your memory for dates. Don't bother to tell us that it happened in—whatever the year was. You needn't try to outsmart Morven now. She's left the field to you."

"It was 1692," Doran said before she could stop herself.

Both men looked at her as though she were something no respectable dog would bother to retrieve. So much for Henry's old admiration, for Dermid's confidences. They only cared for Morven: still.

But Rose licked her hands, looking up at her with adoring amber eyes.

"I knew an awfully nice woman called Campbell," Rodney said. "In my first parish. Active church worker, splendid at raising funds."

Nobody commented. Rodney, Doran, Henry, and Dermid were sitting slumped round what remained of a fire in the Long Drawing Room. The young staff had amazingly slept through it all, Burnelle and Ogle had finally gone back to bed.

Ogle had been furious that Rodney had failed to catch Morven in her headlong flight. "A self-confessed double murderer and you let her get away—in a stolen car at that!"

"Her legs are younger than mine," Rodney replied mildly, "and I slipped in the slush outside the front door. Sorry."

"And it's hardly Mr. Chelmarsh's job to chase criminals," Burnelle reminded his superior. "If even one of us had been there when she ran for it she wouldn't have had a chance."

"I doubt that," said Doran. "She ran like a fiend. Literally." Rodney and she exchanged glances. *A phantasm in the habit of a fair gentlewoman*, Lamia's description in the Latin story.

Ogle glared at her. "If you hadn't been careless enough to leave your keys in the ignition she wouldn't have got away in your car. Bloody stupid thing to do, if I may say so."

Doran glared back. "It may have been stupid but it seems to me excusable, after the weather conditions we've had. I was astonished that my car even started for me, let alone for someone who didn't know its ways."

Ogle grunted. "We'll get her tonight, anyway. She'll have to stop for medical help with that wound in her leg." The young policemen had with great difficulty managed to start another car and were now on the track of Harris and Morven. They might even have caught up with her by now, but somehow Doran doubted it. She noted cynically that Ogle had not volunteered to go with them on their unpleasant journey— Sam, the local bobby, had been good enough for that.

In Morven's room they had found Reg Haslem's driving licence, credit cards, car keys and assorted effects. His pockets had been very efficiently frisked after he was dead.

They also found a photograph, the full-length portrait of a young man in Highland costume. The slightly turned head was beautifully shaped, the hair short and curling, eyes and mouth at once beguiling and mocking.

"I see what she meant," said Doran. "Another deadly charmer, Angus."

Now they were alone together, the four of them. Dermid seemed on the edge of collapse, Henry all of ten years older than his age. It seemed callous to question them, but Doran would never have another chance. She said to Henry, "You did tell me a lot of lies, you know."

"Not a single one."

"Well, you implied things. You gave me the impression that you weren't interested in Morven. You hardly looked at her or spoke to her. I asked you if you'd—er—wooed her, and you said you hadn't tried very hard. Oh. Obviously not, if she gave in the first time."

"She did. I was a useful instrument for her. I lived with her, on and off, though I never in fact stayed with her overnight, that way she kept her independence."

Dermid put his head in his hands.

"Just Visiting, as they say in Monopoly," Doran reflected. To Henry she said, "But if you'd already—er—won her, why did it all matter so much? I mean, why did you risk your integrity and your professional reputation over that fake jewel? You laid it all on the line, and for what?"

"To keep her. She promised that if I helped her bring it off she'd marry me, or live with me on a permanent basis. Sorry, Dermid."

"She wouldn't have kept her promise," Dermid said dully. "She cared too much about her fag of a husband. He was the only thing she *did* care about—enough to cheat and murder. The only thing she was passionate about."

"Still the blood is warm, the heart is Highland," Rodney murmured. "Quite a relief to know she was human."

Doran had been adding things up. "I suppose that was why she was so upset when Howell told us about Lydgate's unpleasant—well, the company he kept."

"She was sickened," Dermid said. "To think that Angus was mixed up with that sort of stuff. Still is, obviously. She'd thought—oh God, she was a romantic, whatever you may think of her. I've had enough of this, I'm going to bed."

Henry stood up. "I've got some sleeping pills. Would you like one? It might help."

Dermid managed something like a smile. "Thanks. I'd knock myself out with brandy, but I'm not supposed to drink, though why it should matter now I don't know, I don't care if I kill myself."

The two men went out together; both defeated. Rivals and undeclared enemies so short a time ago, yet the older man seemed suddenly to have become friend and protector to the younger.

"Don't worry about them," Rodney said. "They'll get over it. The fact of someone being a murderer can have a very powerful effect, even on the infatuated. They must have guessed she'd killed twice, but neither of them would face up to it. I think it may have dinted her image in their hearts, whatever they may feel now, and they obviously feel a great deal. The late Lydgate doesn't sound to me a great loss to the human race, and I shouldn't think the saints have taken a fancy to him at all. But the unfortunate Haslem seems to have been an innocent, so far as any of us are. And people shouldn't go round knocking off other people, by *skean-dhus* or otherwise, it shows a want of sensibility. How did you get on to the *skean-dhu*, by the way?"

"The old Chesterton thing, the dagger of ice, I suppose. Lydgate was killed with a sharp instrument, no such sharp instrument could be found. I knew I'd seen something of the kind and remembered where. A Highland should wear it in the top of his stocking, of course, but as that wasn't practicable Morven calmly sported it in her kilt, where it was rather conspicious to a trained female eye. And speaking of Chesterton—she was a Catholic. How does that fit in?"

"Oh, quite well. She'll go to Confession on Saturday and the priest will say, Tut, tut, twenty-five Aves to be said every half hour and *Father, I have sinnéd* a hundred times in your best writing. No, I'm being most unfair. If he's any good he'll put the fear of God into her—not before time. Or the fear of hellfire."

Doran yawned and stood up. The portrait of the skating charmer looked down, inscrutably coy.

"I shall never know what she's saying. Oh, Mr. Chalon, how you do throw a girl into a flutter, perhaps? Or something more sinister? I still think she was a Lamia, like Morven."

"Who, exactly as Keats said, vanished with a frightful

scream. Though not, in Lamia's case, from feeling a Labrador bitch's teeth meeting in her calf.''

"Yes, that *was* curious, Rose's attack. The gentlest of dogs. She must have sensed evil—and I think she was quite fond of me. But then she seems fond of everybody." She yawned again. Rodney put his arm round her shoulders.

"*I'm* quite fond of you. I wouldn't have gone chasing after Morven if I hadn't known that you were all right. Come on, time we were in bed."

The Manor settled itself down for the night. It still contained a corpse, but it had contained many in its time, as it had contained living people feeling the emotions of its inhabitants tonight: disappointed passion, self-disgust, suicidal despair, wedded love.

And frustrated ambition. The telephone rang in Ogle's ear, shocking him awake.

"Yes?"

"Ride here, sir." The voice was weary. "We haven't caught up with her, she's got clean away."

"I don't believe you. How did you let that happen, you bloody fools?"

"The engine stalled. We're stuck, miles from anywhere. We shan't be able to get away till morning."

Ogle slammed the receiver back into its cradle and uttered all the worst words he knew. They made an impressive collection.

Chapter 13

The flower will bloom another year

A night of steady thaw produced a morning world of slush. The dazzle of white had given way to something resembling a bad etching of a country scene. Roofs were still piebald, part snowy, part bare, gutters douched the unwary with icy dollops, fences reappeared like exhumed blackened bones, trees shed their icing sugar and returned to being gaunt silhouettes on which disgruntled birds sat in rows waiting for food.

In the drive forms wearing a variety of borrowed boots worked on cars, scraping off caked snow and freeing wheels from the morass. Doran and Rodney helped to get Howell's car fit for the road, since they would need it to get home.

"If I hadn't cleared Harris that bent woman wouldn't have had a cat's chance in Hell," Howell mused.

"No. I just wish it hadn't been Harris she took. He was so nice and new, and she's bound to crash him or dump him in a ditch." Those small, steel-strong hands which had been ready to choke the life out of Doran would have no mercy on her car, once it had served its purpose.

Not to mention the blood on the upholstery.

"Look." Rodney pointed to where an ambulance was lumbering awkwardly up the carriage road, a police car stumbling in its wake. The police on the spot had briskly mobilized themselves to leave, as they had come, by the helicopter, on which the young pilot was working.

The officers who had gone in chase of Morven had finished up by plodding to a farmhouse, Burnelle said. It was not far from the main road to Maidstone, from which town a car would be collecting them.

The two senior officers approached on their way to the helicopter pad. Ogle went by without a word—he had not forgiven Doran for unwittingly letting her car become an escape vehicle. Burnelle paused.

"Sam Eastry said to tell you he's going straight home."

"Oh, is he?" The information meant nothing to Doran on the face of it. "Why did he specially want me to know?"

"No idea, I'm afraid."

Rodney came round the back of the car. "I heard that. You don't suppose Sam's been told something we haven't? About Helena, for instance?"

"I'm sure he hasn't." But she was not sure at all.

"Something up with Helena?" Howell asked, hopefully. He detested the girl who had given Doran so much aggro. A glance at Rodney persuaded him that it would be wiser not to dilate on the subject, but it rejoiced him to think of Helena falling headlong into a snowdrift and never getting out any more.

An engine woke into life: the Blatts' Mercedes, starting to cheers from John and Terry, who had between them got it going. Mr. Blatt graciously felt in his pocket for a fiver. It was a lot to part with, but worth it to get away from this dangerous house. John and Terry thankfully gave the Merc a last push as it started on the first stage of its journey to London.

The boys had got Henry's Audi going, too. Henry and Dermid, ready to leave, paused on their way to it.

"Well," Henry said, "goodbye." Rodney tactfully wandered off towards the house.

"Goodbye," Doran said, cheerfully. There was really nothing else to say after what had happened—and not happened. Loyally, she had told the police nothing about Henry's part in the production of the Saxon jewel. If Morven were caught, and talked, that would be something else, but Henry had suffered enough already, in her opinion.

He produced something from his pocket. It lay in his gloved palm, a sunny gleam of bright gold and painted enamel. Aelhswith the False.

"What will you do with it?" Doran asked.

"Keep it in a display case. It'll be a most salutary reminder of—a number of things. To be a fool may be forgivable, but to be a criminal fool . . . I shall take whatever's coming to me, you know."

"I hope it won't," Doran said sincerely.

"Thank you. As soon as this blasted weather clears I'm taking Dermid to Switzerland. A friend of mine has a unique horological collection I think he ought to see, at a château just on the Liechtenstein border."

Howell leaned eagerly across the bonnet. "Oh, whereabouts? Is it open to anyone?"

"Never you mind," Doran told him.

Dermid actually smiled. "I'd rather like it if Howell came with us."

There was the least of pauses on Henry's part before he said, "Of course. Want to think about it, Howell? This is my card—give me a ring in town."

Howell beamed, for once short of words. Someone actually wanted him. He would be good for Dermid, burning enthusiast as he was for his own line.

"Goodbye again," Henry said. He picked up Doran's hand, grimed from the car, and kissed it. They might never meet again, and perhaps that was a good thing, but as he walked away she felt a distinct, curious pang of something she preferred not to identify. The leonine head, white as the snows which were melting, disappeared behind a windscreen and the car door slammed. Doran went hurriedly off towards the house. Her bag was in the hall. And there was never any point in seeing people off.

As the car ground, slithered and faltered its way down the carriage road, Doran turned to look back at the house. Plain, severe, aloof, it seemed not to bend the gaze of its windows on the scurrying figures in front of it, but to stare thoughtfully over the lake and the meadow-grounds. Perhaps it looked back to the man who pulled down its Plantagenet bricks and rebuilt it as Queen Anne would approve, or to his son who bestowed much cost in "improving" it to the taste of George I.

Would it, Doran wondered, have frowned on that later family who ripped out its Chinese Chippendale staircase, and casually used bits of it around the outhouses and stables? Almost certainly. And did it value the Tudor panels of the inner hall, with their Emblems of the Passion, brought to it from an ancient chapel?

Rodney startled her by following her thoughts, as he sometimes did.

"Mary Honeywood owned that chapel," he said.

"How did you know I was . . . never mind. Who was Mary Honeywood?"

"A lady who left 376 living descendants."

"Good heavens."

"She had, as the saying goes, not been idle . . . One of them remembered a dinner she gave at which two hundred persons sat down. I wonder if she borrowed the Manor for it?"

"If she did, I bet the service wasn't as slick as it is now. Did you tip those girls, by the way?"

"Of course. Tiggy."

"Acksherly.

"Acksherly. For all of them. I felt as if I were trying to

tip royalty, but she took it as graciously as though it were she who was bestowing the favour. Charming creature.''

They turned the corner of the lane, and the Manor vanished from their sight. The car began to pick its way through the village, whose inhabitants were vigorously and virtuously sweeping and digging clear paths to their doors. A lot of the displaced slush had ended up in the road, rendering it comfortably passable for a bicycle, barely so for a car. Howell made a great many observations in Welsh. Rodney gave thanks that he was not driving.

The lanes beyond the village were comparatively easy going—the Triceratops and its relations and friends had been at work. In a few covered pens sheep nibbled fodder, their fleeces dirty-yellow as old ivory against the untouched snow of the meadows.

Another village: Doran recognized the cobbled square and the church which had attracted her as she drove to the Manor.

"I looked it up," she told Rodney. "It's got a sort of bishop's armchair and a painting of St. Michael weighing souls in a kitchen scale."

"I know," Rodney sounded abstracted. "And the prolific Mary Honeywood's buried there. She's mentioned in Foxe's Book of Martyrs, by the way."

"Not surprising, after having all those children."

"It wasn't for that, in fact, but because she lost a shoe going home from seeing a Protestant burned. Curious way of getting into the annals of Foxe . . ."

Doran stole a glance at his profile. He was talking for the sake of talking, as she was.

" 'Ere we go,'' grunted Howell. They were coming up to the main road, where a dense line of traffic was visible at the T-junction, not so much crawling as stationary. "This is it, folks, unfasten your seatbelts and get ready for a long sit. Wish I'd got my bottle with me.''

"We're extremely grateful that you haven't,'' Doran said.

191

"I was just thinking how beautifully you were driving, so calm, so masterful, so . . ."

"Austere," Rodney suggested. "Stately. Graceful and swanlike. We do admire you so much, Howell."

"Compliments'll get you nowhere. Nothing'll get you anywhere, in this lot. Look at it, soddin' look at it!"

A double line of vehicles extended, apparently, from Maidstone to the coast: saloon cars, farm lorries, Continental transports driven by men whose phlegmatic expressions suggested resignation to the fact that Albion's perfidy extended to its weather. The car's interior was very cold, but when Howell turned on the heater it created a miasma of stale smoke, departed liquor, uncleaned upholstery and fish: Howell, like other Eastgateians, often went down to the beach to buy cheaply from a new-landed catch.

Doran wished the old custom of carriage rugs still prevailed in cars. She tried holding Rodney's hand, but somehow it failed to warm her. Instead she tucked hers into the deep pocket of his coat.

It was impossible to sit in silence, in an almost motionless car. Especially after the hectic two days they had just spent.

"I wonder how far Morven got," she said.

Howell turned his head. "Bloody lucky to get over the county border, in this."

"I wouldn't be too sure," mused Rodney. "Rather more than capable, that lady, in conditions which would daunt other people."

"Did you sense evil in her?" Doran asked. "That crucifix of yours must have given a twitch or two when you first met her."

"Difficult question, that. Curiously enough, not actual evil, no. Something else, perhaps. Pride, overweening pride? *By that sin fell the angels.* It can make mortals feel more than mortal, as I think she did. It was just a pity she didn't or

192

couldn't deal with her enemies by something other than murder, since she obviously had powers of a sort."

"The serpent only strikes when it's attacked, and then people blame it and call it names."

"I wonder what will happen to Morven when they catch her, as they undoubtedly will?"

"Medical and psychological reports," said Doran. "Defence counsel will do its best to prove that she wasn't in her right mind, Prosecution will point to all her degrees and qualifications to prove that she was, and the final result will probably be a spell of remedial treatment and a token year or so in one of those open prisons."

"Not Broadmoor? I hope not Broadmoor. She is, after all, a thing of beauty, and institutions for the criminally insane are hardly calculated to preserve someone as a joy forever."

"Isn't it extraordinary how Keats has sort of dominated this affair, from St. Agnes's Eve onwards," Doran mused.

"Amazing—it isn't just me, being tiresomely literary. Don't you think the essence of it has been the line everybody knows, even if they can't quote another thing he said—*Beauty is Truth, Truth Beauty*? Morven was superbly beautiful, so a man married her who had no business to be married at all—"

"And Henry was prepared to sacrifice himself totally for her, and Dermid was prepared to die for love as well as lie for it, and so two men were murdered and I nearly was, and the antiques trade nearly had the fake of the century perpetrated on it. That's right. The truth lay in Morven's beauty. Well, well."

"Mind you," Rodney said, "I always thought that line was a bit specious. He wasn't much more than a boy when he wrote it, and if he'd lived I fear he'd have found that beauty was anything but a universal truth . . ."

Doran felt in her shoulder-bag for the little notebook in which she had started jotting down fascinating facts, such as

193

this aphorism, in case she should ever get tired of dealing and write a book. The notebook had slipped down into that almost unfathomable space between purse compartment and the base of the bag, where it was hiding coyly among keys, two handkerchieves, a lipstick, a case for sunglasses which had no business to be there at all in January, an empty phial of cologne, and the little box which contained her magnifying glass.

Her seeking fingers paused, as an icy chill flooded her veins. Another little box, which should have been there, was not there.

She had left home in a hurry and a temper. Carole's arrival had interrupted her packing. They had discussed Helena's pills. Helena's pills. But her own, essential pillbox was in a bedside drawer.

And last night she had forgotten, swept away in the relief of sharing the Victorian double bed with Rodney.

The small sound of distress she made was lost on Rodney, who was wandering gently in the hinterland of Keats's juvenile verse.

"I suppose it was all the frightful things he'd seen in the hospitals that inspired him to write of Woman *God, she is like a milk-white lamb that bleats*. And his ear for rhyme wasn't entirely perfect when he rhymed *sobbings* with *mournful robins*—not that robins *are* mournful, in any case, quite the reverse . . ."

Doran sat beside him as cold as if she had been up to her neck in the frozen slush which lined each side of the road. I could have a baby. Not for certain, because of the buildup protection, but I might. What would that do to us, with Helena's mad jealousy? She could do it some awful injury—kill it, perhaps. There was a story about her being cruel to a kitten at the vicarage . . .

And Rodney. They'd been fighting about that very subject the night before she had left for the Manor. "You can hardly blame me for not wanting a child of my own when I've got a stepchild like Helena,'' she had said—or words to that effect. Rodney wanted a child of hers, no doubt of that, but he knew quite well what it would do to their lives.

She wanted one herself, very much. She couldn't possibly get rid of it, of a life, a life that she and Rodney had created.

She and Rodney. A new, even more awful thought struck her. If she and Henry, the other night . . . if she had not been half-drunk, and Henry kind and chivalrous. A deep shudder shook her.

"You're not getting a chill, are you?'' Rodney asked. "Howell, there's nowhere we could stop for coffee, is there?''

Howell gave a cynical hoot of laughter. Doran fixed her eyes on the back of his head. The car was moving a shade faster, the monotonous passing of vehicles on each side of it making her feel sick, even more sick than she felt already. She leaned against Rodney's shoulder and shut her eyes.

It helped the nausea, but not the black thoughts in her head. Helena. She was unlike herself, Vi had said. Her voice had been weak, without its sharp edge. Suppose, in her frail state, she had caught a germ which would kill her: suppose she died? If she dies I shall feel I've wished it on her, because I have, sometimes, in my wicked moments . . .

Rodney had stopped talking. She knew that he was thinking along similar lines. What would they find at home? How sad, to dread coming home . . .

The black thoughts merged into wilder, random ones, nonsense scenes and visions. She slept uneasily against Rodney's shoulder. Looking down, he saw the unhappy line of her mouth, and the frown between her brows; and was troubled.

"Not far now.'' Howell's voice woke her to the realization that they were away from the congested main road, moving at a fair speed on the broad lane which led into their valley.

There was the witch-house with the crooked chimney, on the other side of the fine old barn and the half-timbered farm-house. There was the small Saxon church of St. Eanswythe, now used as a youth centre, its gravestones white mounds of set snow.

And, astonishingly soon, there was the beautiful stout-panther bulk of the Rose Reviv'd, Abbotsbourne's pub-restaurant, and Rosie Bellacre, its landlady, sweeping snow outside the front door. She straightened and waved to the car, good-natured creature that she was. Then the right-hand turn down into the village square, the greengrocer's, the post office with a banner-poster outside saying SNOW CHAOS, the three-cornered cottage and the turn into Mays Lane.

"We're here," Rodney said. "Wake up."

Bell House sat sedately in its snow-smothered gardens, Queen Anne brick and nine front windows calmly braced against whatever assaults might come. As they stopped in the drive a figure unfolded itself from behind the party hedge between Bell House and Magnolia House, its newer neigh-bour: a tall slim figure clad in ski-wear which would not have disgraced royalty.

"Hullo," said Richenda Berg, "you're back, then."

Doran climbed stiffly out of the passenger seat, surprised to find herself able to move without creaking audibly. Ri-chenda's bright blonde hair was invisible beneath a tight cap of azure wool which set off her sapphire eyes, perfectly false-lashed and ochre-shaded at four o'clock on a dark winter afternoon. Her face was a delicate toast-brown.

"So are you, I see," replied Doran. "I thought you were off skiing." (With a young chap not half her age, Vi had mentioned.)

"There wasn't enough snow on the slopes—boring. Comic, too, when you look at this lot. So I came back. Cosmo's in Australia." She spoke to Doran but the sapphires were beamed on Rodney, lecherously, Doran was sure. But

196

he was concerned with the car and the problem of the snow-blocked garage. Richenda waved vaguely and sank out of sight again after a raking glance which took in Howell, sampled and dismissed him.

The kitchen was blessedly warm and tidy. Tybalt, respectably curled up in his basket, opened one green eye at them and shut it again. If there was guilt on his conscience it didn't show.

Vi appeared from the wash-house, a basket of folded linen classically balanced on one ample hip.

"Oh, you got back, then. Thought you might not get through till tonight. Terrible, isn't it, worse than when it was snowing, really, I thought about you a lot. Good afternoon, Mr. Evans. Stopping off, are you? I'll get the spare room ready."

"I think he'll have to stop," Doran said, "as we've only one car between us—mine was stolen. Please, please may we have some tea, Vi, and whatever you've got to eat? We haven't eaten since breakfast and we're famished out of our minds—at least, I am."

"So am I," Rodney said. "I won't say I could eat a horse, but if one put its head round the door I might be very tempted to ask it in." Howell added that his stomach thought his throat had been cut.

"Right." Vi enjoyed demands on her resources. "I'll get the big teapot down, the brown one with them pretty raised flowers all over it, and you could have eggs on toast with bacon and beans or I'll do a proper mixed grill if you like, it's just as easy. I made a pie yesterday because there was some apples still in the loft, but there's no cream, they just can't get any. You go and change, now, and I'll lay it out in here where it's warm."

Doran looked lovingly round her pretty kitchen, the Minton tiles decorated with strapping Victorian fairies and elves, the Staffordshire figures on the dresser, Prince Albert, Jenny

Lind, Uncle Tom and Little Eva, Maria Marten being murdered in the Red Barn, and the rather naughty Rowlandson print which Vi primly never glanced at. How delightful to see all the homely things again, after the sinister splendours of the Manor. If only she could forget her tensions and enjoy it all . . .

"How's Helena?" Rodney asked. "In bed, I suppose."

"Not that I know of. She was in her room, mending something or other, last I saw of her."

"Oh. But I thought you said she'd caught the current bug."

"She sounded very odd on the phone," said Doran.

"Oh yes. Well. She's a funny little thing."

Funny? It was not the adjective either would have applied to Helena.

"Come on," Rodney said. As they went towards the old rooms which were Helena's, still in their coats and wraps, Doran wished that she had been able to snatch a cup of tea first, before this encounter. But better to get it over and done with.

Helena looked up from the sewing basket on her lap, from which bright skeins of wool were spilling. On the table was what Doran recognized as the hassock-cover she had started working on, as a gesture towards being the perfect vicar's wife.

"Hello," Helena said. She was not scowling. She seemed not to be ill at all. "I wondered how you were getting on—I kept listening to the radio and it said the roads were awful."

Rodney dropped a kiss on her hair. "They were. Much have we travelled in the realms of slush. How've you been?"

"Oh, I'm all right, Daddy. I thought I'd get on with your hassock, Doran, as there's no school. It's quite an easy pattern, isn't it?" She displayed the cross-stitch design of the Fish, the most ancient Christian symbol. There was a lot more of it than when Doran had seen it last.

"That's . . . very thoughtful of you, Helena. Actually

198

you're better at it than I am." With those slightly deformed hands and bent shoulders, so that it wasn't possible to sit up straight with one's embroidery.

A small silence fell. Then Helena put the sewing basket on the table, clasped her hands and looked from one face to the other.

"I want to say something to you. I'm very sorry. I've been a beast to you both, especially you, Doran. I knew I was doing it but somehow I couldn't stop, and I felt I had to go on because you expected it . . . oh, I don't know how to explain."

"Don't try," said Rodney gently.

"Yes, I must, Daddy. You see, I was dreadfully jealous of Doran because I thought you were the only person who'd ever love me, and because you loved her I thought you couldn't love me as much. I know that's silly, Annabella explained it to me."

Doran swallowed. "Annabella?"

"My great friend. Her family moved to Elvesham last term. We've been having long phone talks since school closed—I knew you wouldn't mind, even if it cost a lot. Annabella's so clever, *brilliant*, everyone thinks so, and absolutely gorgeous—that Mrs. Berg next door isn't anything like so beautiful, and anyway it's all makeup," added Helena with a flash of the old malice. "Isn't it wonderful that a Senior like Annabella should make a friend of *me*? But she really is my friend, she says I'm clever and even rather . . . nice-looking, if I didn't frown so much. (Anyway, it makes lines on your face.) And she says I ought to go to your Confirmation classes with her, Daddy."

"Good. Good," said Rodney feebly.

Helena's cheeks were pink with the effort she had summoned up, her hair, for once, brushed smooth. She was indeed rather nice-looking now that her expression matched the delicate features.

"And Annabella says that you've been much kinder to me than I deserved, Doran, and put up with a lot, because she's heard the way I've spoken to you at school. And I do like you, really I do—I think you're very clever, and—and very pretty. It's only that I was jealous."

"I know that," Doran said. She and Rodney employed their private, silent communication signals. I'm going to play this very calmly, she told him. No fuss, no emotional scene— just acceptance. And Rodney's eyes answered that she was absolutely right, it was precisely his own plan.

"Well," Doran said, "I think that sorts us out very nicely, Helena, and thank you for saying it. I really do like you, too—it's all been a nonsense, hasn't it? I don't expect you to look on me as a mother, that would be ridiculous—perhaps you could think of me as a sort of honorary Senior, like Annabella?"

"Yes!" Helena's dark eyes were bright with pleasure. "Yes, I will. Can I ring her now to tell her it worked? Being truthful, I mean."

"Of course," Rodney said. "Feel free—take all evening, if you like."

"Except for having tea with us first," Doran added. "We're just going to wash and change and then we'll all have it in the kitchen. You'll need more of that red wool—I'll walk down to the square and get some tomorrow." She touched Rodney's arm and went out of the room.

He followed her along the hall and upstairs to their room before he spoke.

"It's incredible, marvellous. I almost don't believe it."

"I don't know what to believe. Can it possibly last?"

"I think so. These things happen in the most extraordinary way. It's Love's Awakening, isn't it: I mean love in its most basic sense. *Agape* to the Greeks. *Caritas* to the Romans. An older girl she admires to the point of adoration, coming into her life just at the right adolescent moment."

"I know, I remember it. In my case it was a really very plain girl called Johnson with a slight Yorkshire accent."

"Exactly. Annabella's probably quite ordinary, it's all in the eye of the beholder. And when Annabella's sweet Pleiadic influence wears off there'll be somebody else—almost certainly male next time."

"I remember that too. Our fishmonger's son. His name was Frank."

"*Schwärmerei,* young hero-worship. Perhaps what Keats meant by *the holiness of the heart's affections.* Doran, I'm so thankful, so grateful."

Doran nodded. She was beyond telling him how grateful she was herself. She sat down and began to peel off her damp boots, in a half-dream.

"I've just remembered," Rodney said. "Tomorrow's the eve of the Conversion of St. Paul. *He came near Damascus, and suddenly there shined about him a light from Heaven.*"

"St. Agnes and St. Paul. What a very, very curious week." Doran was standing by the window, looking down at the garden.

"Come here," she said. "See. There, where the snow's been cleared away from the border."

"I can't see anything special." Rodney adjusted his spectacles.

"Snowdrops. *The first snowdrop of the year, That in my bosom lies.*" She turned in the circle of his arm. "Another odd thing—that's out of another poem called *St. Agnes' Eve,* by I forget whom."

"I don't, for once, care," said Rodney, and kissed her.

The telephone rang. It was Sam Eastry.

"They've found your car. It was in a car park in Bromley, very neatly parked. No damage, no clues—and no sign of the lady. Rather a lot of bloodstains, though, it'll need professional cleaning. Somebody's driving it back tomorrow, when the roads are clearer. Thought you'd like to know.''

"I'm delighted, Sam. Dear Harris, I've missed him. As for Mrs. Cair, she's probably been spirited back to her dusky brake. I'm sure Lamia turned back into a serpent.''

"Beg your pardon, Doran, didn't quite hear.''

"Never mind. You got back all right?''

"Fine. I was a bit jumpy at the Manor, wanted to get home. In fact, there's something else you might like to know. Lydia's expecting a baby. She's all right, they're both going to be all right—she's just had a scan, because of her age, and it's a girl.''

Doran said everything the ecstatic father wanted to hear, which was a lot. Difficult, since she was almost speechless with happiness.

From the kitchen floated a savoury fragrance of cooking, but she lingered at the hall window. The snowdrops were still there.

Shed no tear, O shed no tear: the flower will bloom another year.